Pippin Pearmain has a screen test — the first in several years. Before flying to Sydney to meet her new agent, the director, and the rest of the cast of *Half-Life of the Lost*, she cashes in the mystery holiday voucher that was a gift from her recently deceased Cousin Lupin. Sailing on the yacht *Tulpenmanie* was fun . . . until one of the crewmen went missing. That was bad, but now he's turned up and jumped into the sea with Pip in his arms.

Well . . . she did agree to meet his family!

Skinny dipping under a waterfall, swimming into a cave, dancing on the chalk and meeting an extended family takes Pip's mind off the impending return to film work, but even holidays in fairyland have to end. Pip knows she needs to be back at Lemonwood Cottage in time to take her agent's call. She has to organise a sitter for the cats who seemed curiously willing to let her go and leave them with a stranger.

Pippin Pearmain has led an interesting life, but it had been winding down. Now, at the age of sixty-six, that life has gone utterly nuts.

She wouldn't change that for the world.

Performing Pippin Pearmain 3
Copyright © 2023 Lark Westerly
ISBN: 978-1-4874-3713-8
Cover art by Martine Jardin

Published by eXtasy Books Inc

Look for us online at:
www.eXtasybooks.com

Performing Pippin Pearmain 3
Performing Pippin Pearmain

By

Lark Westerly

DEDICATION

For lovers of beautiful places who dance or swim and embrace the unexpected.

AUTHOR'S NOTE

Fiction and Reality

Major places in this story, such as Tasmania, the city of Sydney, and the state of Victoria are real, and if you visit them, you'll find them more or less as represented here. Bass Strait is real, and beautiful, and wet. The towns of Jellico Bay and Delmsford are inventions, as is Delphinium Island. And yet . . . there *are* small, quaint towns in Tasmania with retro pubs and festival venues that are quite a big deal. The Vouch-Safe company doesn't exist in our world. I wish it did, so it popped up in some of my earlier titles. Who wouldn't want an Experience tailored to their tastes and inner personalities? No planning, no organising, no spending hours on hold or trying to find flights or venues or vendors . . . just get in a car and relax until it's time to have that adventure.

Pip's story covers a year, taking her from her reclusive cottage in Jellico Bay to her old hometown of Delmsford, to the magical fossmere, on to Sydney and thence to Delphinium Island and beyond. The nine books of *Performing Pippin Pearmain* compile into one continuing story, slowly revealing the mystery and magic that has been part of Pip's world all along.

And how did I come to write Pip's story? It all began in February 2022 with a flower show . . . and with a bucket.

The story so far . . .

Book One

Introducing Pippin Pearmain — small, eccentric, determined, sixty-six, and ruled by cats. Until a decade ago, Pip earned her living by playing offbeat roles on stage and screen, but after her mother and her agent died in the same week, the work dried up and she moved to Jellico Bay. During a visit to her old hometown she encountered her cousins, Lupin de Leon and Juniper "Jan" Sharman. They, and Jan's daughter, Clarkia, were the only remaining members of the Laurel-Pearmain-de-Leon family. Over afternoon tea at the Delmsford Flower Show, Pip revealed her long-held secret — her bucket list — a literal list of interesting buckets. In return, her cousins wrote down their secrets.

Home in her cottage with the original cat and the back-up cat, which communicate with her in what she thinks of as Cat-Morse, Pip read the secrets. Jan identified herself as the novelist Juniper Gin. Lupin's secret was shocking — she had just a few months to live.

After Lupin's passing, Jan met the cats Kittisack and Amberjill and received a bucket Pip had promised for Lupin's last repose. They discussed the provenance of a family heirloom — two copies of a book called *Grandmother's Sunshine*. Lacking heirs, Pip had once offered her copy to a young friend, whose mother refused to let her accept it. A call from Clarkia prompted Jan to dash off, leaving Pip with Lupin's legacy — an envelope and a pottery cat.

Book Two

Pip received a call from Magda Saxer, announcing herself as Pip's new agent and offering a role in a film called *Half-Life of the Lost*. The cats were unexpectedly in favour. They suggested Jan's daughter would look after them.

Lupin's envelope contained a voucher written in disappearing ink. Pip called the information line, whereupon Gerry Trip, Lupin's ex-colleague at Vouch-Safe, informed her she had one hour to prepare for a mystery Experience.

Gerry's step-grandson, Jamie, promised to cat-sit. He drove Pip to a rendezvous.

Pip boarded the yacht *Tulpenmanie*, crewed by pleasant Zach, his odd girlfriend Jisinia, and Jamie's uncle Tane.

When Pip realised Tane was missing, she called triple zero. Jisinia confiscated the phone but returned it. Pip rationalised that Tane must have returned to shore.

That night, Tane, who was a silversmith, was somehow back on board. After resizing Pip's ring, he invited her to meet his family. She agreed.

Tane picked her up and jumped into the sea.

BOOK THREE

The one you are about to read begins in the ocean, travels to the charming fossmere, and thence to Hob's Island and back to Lemonwood Cottage via the yacht *Tulpenmanie*.

The story continues

PART ONE. OVER THERE

April 2022

CHAPTER ONE. NOT DROWNING

Going dowwwwwwnnnn.

The shock of autumnal water in a stretch of sea never renowned for balmy temperatures should have shocked tiny Pippin Pearmain into silence. She'd never been brave, and she had not much body fat to keep her warm.

A moment ago she'd been aboard the yacht *Tulpenmanie,* enjoying a mystery Experience, an adventure holiday donated by her late Cousin Lupin.

Now . . .

I should never have said I'd come to meet his family!

Bubbles tickled her face and her bare arms. Her head spun off into a fugue of terror which lasted a good five seconds before her old friend Sully's advice seeped into her mind. Sully's sayings were always her safety net through the years of growing up and beyond.

Luv, if any man — or woman — tries anything you don't think is to your benefit, holler out now. Don't ever keep quiet if a hand goes where it shouldn't. Holler now, holler loud, and Sully will get out her nutcrackers.

Sully couldn't get her out of this one. Possibly no one could. A knee where it hurt was one possibility for escaping unwelcome embraces, but Tane had his arm under her knees. Anyway, he wasn't exactly advancing. It was more of an —

The descent slowed and halted. They headed back to the surface.

"Okay lovie?" Tane's tone was light and cheerful — inviting her to share the joke of her third abduction in less than three months. It was becoming a habit.

She'd survived the other two, but this was the strangest yet.

A weird thought struck her. *This is what he is. This is what he does.*

He's half fish, Zach the temporary skipper had said, and *You can't drown Tane,* Zach's girlfriend, Jisinia, had added. *You'll be offered a chance at that extra experience at some point, but you do not have to say yes.* That had been Zach again, or earlier, and he'd sounded worried.

Pip grumbled to herself as she bobbed in the unexpectedly warm ocean in Tane's arms. He was Jamie's *uncle,* for goodness' sake! And Jamie was minding the cats while she was away . . . Jamie was a sweet boy. He was eighteen and *utterly reliable,* according to Gerry Trip.

Tane had given Pip a sorry-for-treading-on-you and getting-to-know-you picnic on the deck of *Tulpenmanie.* It had involved Indian tea and fat fresh figs and a lot of peculiar conversation. Then he'd invited Pip to visit his family. She'd agreed. She hadn't said *no.* She really should have done. Meeting strange men's families was probably not a good idea, yet how could she possibly have guessed saying *yes* would send her overboard?

She said, as nonchalantly as she could manage, "You're awfully buoyant, Tane. Tane what, anyway? Jamie wouldn't tell me his surname and I suppose it's the same as yours. Unless you're his mother's brother, of course."

"I'm Tane Pendennis. I'm his father's semi-brother — we share the same dad. He could charm the birds down from the sky, but I was Mam's idea. She asked Dad for a bit of his time, and he agreed. And I'm buoyant only when I want to be." He expelled some air from his lungs and sank so Pip's chin encountered the choppy little waves of Bass Strait.

"Stop that!" she growled.

He inhaled and the water lapped back at her chest.

2

She worked a hand free and delivered a light slap to his bare shoulder. "I thought we were going in a boat. To see your family. That's what you said—implied."

"That's not possible," he said.

"If it's impossible to visit them, why did you invite me?"

"It's perfectly possible to visit them. It's just not possible to do it by boat. At least, not from here."

"Then how the *dickens* do we visit them? If that *is* where we're going? Unless you have other plans. And you'd jolly well better not. That would be misrepresentation, and that's not *legal*."

He expelled some breath.

Pip hit him again, harder. "Explain yourself or I'll *squeal*."

Tane laughed. He didn't even sound unhinged. "All right, Miss Pearmain. I'm not misrepresenting anything. Here's your explanation. There's a gateway to *over there* out here a little way. We just need to dive to access—"

"Not me. I don't dive. I can. I have. I just don't."

"I mean *I'll* dive to access the gateway. I'll carry you with me. You'll be as safe as anything. *My hand on it*, as my brother Finn says, and when a lad like Finn says that you'd better believe he means it. So do I. We'll go through the gateway, and come up near Hob's Island, or maybe nearer the chalklands would be best. I'll take you to meet my family, as we agreed. Jill will welcome you and give you a cup of tea, and the tiddlers love visitors. *No harm*."

"And if I say *no*? I should have said it before, but I was not put in possession of the facts. I can change my mind if I want."

He sighed. "You are at liberty to change your mind, and to squeal. I'll help you. We can holler in two-part harmony. Jin would hear, and she and Zach could drop the ladder to haul you back aboard. It might take a few minutes to organise your re-embarkation, but I promise you'll come to no harm while we wait."

"What about you?"

"I'd go home as soon as you were on board. Jin's got a nasty tongue on her, and Zach doesn't like it if I use love bubbles to calm her down. Linda did explain to me why I shouldn't do that. *Not appropriate* is the way she put it, but sometimes I forget." He shrugged. "Might as well ask a fish not to swim. Pretending to be something I'm not leads to all sorts of trouble. That's not an excuse. I can't and won't apologise for what I am and what I can't change. Neither should you."

That was something Pip could agree with. "I never have and I never do and I never would."

As for the rest of it . . . *Love bubbles! Fish! And who the hell is Linda?*

"Home as in *down there*. Through your gateway. Under the ocean." Pip used a jerk of her chin to point.

"That's right. We can go *over there*. Heard of it?"

Pip realised with a jolt that she *had* heard of *over there*. It was the way to the *Lovely Land*, the *Fijordlands, Door-in-the-Chalk, Heather Isle, Summer* . . . all settings for delightful stories and verses in *Grandmother's Sunshine*, the book given to one of her ancestors by someone called *Grandmother Aster*. It now belonged to her. She'd only ever seen one other copy besides her own. That one belonged to her cousin Juniper Sharman, who generally preferred to be called Jan.

The magical places in the stories were real in her mind, settled and established in her mental geography since early childhood along with nursery rhymes, the apple tree prince, Ironbark Joe, and all the rich storybook culture provided by the family nannas — all three.

Tane might be using the term figuratively — or not.
Troy turned out to be real. Schliemann went digging for it.
Atlantis never was. Plato made it up.

She pondered her options. Now she was over the initial shock, she really wasn't so scared. No one had ever jumped into the sea with her before, but she *had* been carried off down a ladder and away on a galloping horse in one of her films.

"You're safe with me, Pipkin," Alain, the rider, had said.

Pip had believed him.

On the other hand, Alain had been kind, straightforward, warm, and reliable. He'd smelled of freshly made toast, which was one of Pip's favourite comfort foods.

Tane, on the other hand was definitely slippery, and reputedly impossible to drown. He was *half fish*, as Zach had put it. She gave him a prod in the shoulder to focus his attention.

"You do understand I can't hold my breath for nearly as long as you, right?"

"Obviously you can't," he said.

"I'm fit and healthy, but you're a man, and you're at least a quarter century younger than I am, and you have about forty to sixty percent better lung capacity than me."

"Much more than that, I should think although no one has ever measured it. People like me don't let doctors measure our lung capacity . . . or much else. It only upsets them unless they're from my side of the gates and there aren't too many of those. Don't worry, though. I have enough air in my lungs for both of us."

"And you propose to share this with me—how?"

"How do you think?"

"*I* think if I feel a hand where it ought not to be, or a tongue where—"

"You'll squeal. Or bite."

"Not much point in that. I'll tell your wife and she can take whatever measure she deems fitting to remind you of your manners and your responsibilities. I hope it hurts."

"Good plan," he said, chuckling. "However, it won't be necessary. I will *never* put a hand or a tongue where it ought not to be, on you or anyone else. My beloved will thus never have cause to *take measures*. My hand on it." They bobbed for a few more seconds.

Tulpenmanie was drifting away, presumably under auto-pilot. Much longer, and even a Banshee Mary squeal might not penetrate the chartroom where Zach and Jisinia slept.

"Okay," Pip said, hardly believing her own audacity. "Take us down to your *over there* before I lose my nerve. If you drown me, I give fair warning, there *will* be hell to pay."

In the split second after this pronouncement, she wondered if there really would. She had once been a public figure, sort of, but now, eleven years after her last film, which had made less splash than Tane had when leaping into the ocean, would anyone notice if she *left the building*?

The cats would.

Cats don't report disappearances to the police.

Someone would notice, eventually, when I didn't collect my tarts from Jelly-and-Juice.

She wondered if she'd warrant an inch of column on page 7 or 8.

Former child star disappears.

Concerns are held for the safety of former child actor, Pippin Pearmain. Ms Pearmain, 66, a resident of Jellico Bay, has not been seen since —

Tane's voice interrupted her musing. "In a minute. First . . . I breathe for you. Okay? Don't panic, don't worry, don't gasp or —"

"Get on with it before I change my mind."

Tane said, cheerfully, "I like you a *lot*, Miss Pearmain." Then he bent his head and — at first it felt like a kiss, but Pip soon realised he was doing exactly what he'd proposed — breathing for her.

She fell into his rhythm, just as she had always fallen in with actors in a scene.

Still a quick study, she thought with satisfaction as she accepted the air. Oops. Better not be smug, or the universe will try to drown me to teach me a lesson.

But evidently, the universe had better things to do today.

Or maybe it hadn't noticed her, way out here in the ocean.

Air fizzed through her lungs, tuning up alveoli that had become lazy over the decades. When they felt full, Tane lifted his mouth and said, "Here we go. Breathe out slowly as we go down. I'll give you more when it's needed. I have plenty for us both. Now don't worry *at all*. The first bit's the worst and that's not at all bad. It's even going to be fun if you let it."

His arms tightened, and they sank below the surface.

Pip noted she was not drowning.

She couldn't breathe under water, but it appeared she didn't have to. When they had apparently sunk low enough in the sea, Tane gently released her. Before she had time to panic, he took her hand in the dark. He gave her a gentle tug, and they were off, diving instead of sinking.

I can do this. It's just like riding Varian, with Alain to keep me safe. Just like another performance, but I'm my own audience to my underwater film.

Pip's time sense, never too accurate at the best of times, fuzzed out. She opened her eyes and peered through the depths, but it was dark and all she saw were shifting shadows, black on black. She started to feel dizzy.

Tane evidently noticed because he gave her another air transfusion and they continued through the dark.

After a bit, they stopped, hanging in the water as kites might hang in the air.

"The gate's just ahead," Tane said. His voice bubbled and boomed, but Pip made out the sense of it. She didn't try to speak in return but squeezed his hand in response.

"Stay level with me so you don't scrape the rock going through. It's smooth, but it might knock you sideways."

She squeezed again.

The swell of the ocean rocked her, but she felt safe—just as she had felt safe on the horse Varian's back during the single take of Marigold's abduction by the highwayman when she'd acted in *The House of Heriot*.

Single takes were so rarely enough in a film, but Varian and his master, Alain Barfleur, worked in harmony and all tiny Pippin Pearmain had to do was to sit side-saddle in warm and friendly arms and to allow her body to sway with the galloping motion.

"I've got you, Pipkin." Alain had said it in just such a cheerful tone as Tane employed. "You're safe with me, and with Varian."

He *had* got her, and in some ways he'd never let her go.

They'd ridden again along the beach for another scene in the film. Pip had loved it so much it had frightened her. She'd hoped for more riding roles, preferably with Alain, but they'd never come up. The closest had been in *Gypsy Summer,* where she'd ridden in a painted varda pulled by a patient mare named Evadne.

Her character's name had been Walnut Wednesday, and she'd played the role in brown-face.

Wouldn't fly now. Or would it?

It had been Wednesday Crocker, the runaway socialite, who had stained her face and arms with walnut juice and stolen a summer right under the nose of her minders.

It wasn't me browning my skin to appropriate a culture. It was Wednesday, hiding her identity by pretending to be someone else. Tilly Lovell even helped her with the browning. Might as well complain about women playing in breeches roles.

Mind you, the actor playing Tilly hadn't been a traveller either . . . Cherry Pye had been her name, and she'd assured Pip it was her real one. Her parents had been having a bit of a moment.

Pip felt Tane reach forward, pause, and swim onwards, towing her like the tail of a kite.

A strange bursting sensation startled her, and for a split second she thought they'd broken the surface. She almost gasped, but Tane jack-knifed to circumvent her discomfort with another puff of friendly air.

The water quality had changed. Clear and clean, it was more like liquid air.

Up they went, slowly, with Tane lazily kicking for them both. When they reached the true surface, he pulled her back into his arms.

"Okay, lovie?"

Pip spluttered, mostly for effect, and gulped in an unassisted breath. "Yes."

She used the pause to rub water out of her eyes and to push back her hair, which felt distractingly like wet cottonwool.

In her imagination's eye, she saw herself looking like an ethereal mermaid in the arms of a handsome triton. In her mind's eye, she knew she must look bedraggled. *A drowned rat,* as her old agent, Sully, might have said.

Sully had told her she had magic in her aura. She'd also told her when she needed to brush her hair or put on a hat.

"Those directors like your porcelain skin, so don't go getting tan marks on your ears."

Sully had called a spade a spade and sometimes a bloody shovel, especially when the director wanted Pip to *go and get a suntan before we do the walnut scene.*

Sully had said that was bloody preposterous, so Pip hadn't.

Pip grumbled under her breath. She'd worn an extra-long T-shirt in faded hue of lichen green to sleep in on *Tulpenmanie.* She hadn't expected to wear it visiting.

Tell no one, Kittisack's Cat-Morse would warn . . . But Kittisack wasn't here.

"Where are we?" she asked.

Might as well make the best if it. Can't worry about what I can't change and all that. Besides . . .

The tingle of anticipation made her feel alive.

It was night, but a faint radiance hung about the sea. Pip saw pale cliffs rising not far away.

Tane said, "Those are the cliffs leading to the chalklands. Hob's Island is behind us. It's a nice place. I'll take you there, if you want, or we could go straight to Fosscot — the place I live with my family most of the time."

"I like islands," she said. "Your family will be asleep, right?"

"Sun's rising soon, and the baby's a lark," he said. "Night owl too, of course. Babbies run on their own sweet clocks, as my mammy says. Mind, Mam has probably never seen a clock in her life. Dandelion clock, maybe."

"Let's go and meet the family, then. Maybe I can see the island later."

"I'll make sure to take you there."

"Like this?" She splashed at the water.

He laughed. "No, Miss Pearmain. I'll take you to the island in Hob's boat. *He* won't mind. He's blood-tied with Linda, who is wed to my big semi-brother. Of course he'll lend me his boat. I *could* get it now, but it might take a while. Can you swim to the cliffs under your own steam?"

Pip gauged the distance. *Not so far.* "I think so, but I won't be as fast as you."

"That's not a problem. We'll take all the time we need. Let's go."

He relinquished her to the water, waiting while she oriented herself into a sidestroke position.

She'd always been proficient at swimming, although not as good as Big Nanna de Leon who bobbed about in her vast floral swimsuit while Lupin, Jan, and Pip played around her in Jack Kelly Lake where they'd holidayed. Big Nanna had an interesting and eclectic taste in destinations, and it was never the same place twice.

Tane started out swimming, not Australian Crawl, the favoured show-off stroke of most Australian men, but a fluid motion almost like a dolphin.

Pip followed, taking it easy, but enjoying the weightlessness and unexpected warmth of the water.

This is me, not drowning.

She thought somewhat maliciously of the horror in Kittisack's face if he could see her now.

You're all wet. You stay away from me!

Chapter Two. The Cliff Path

When they reached the cliffs, Tane asked courteously if Pip needed help to climb the path.

Pip did. She was confident about the climb *after* she attached herself to the path, but she didn't feel equal to the propulsion needed to reach it from the water.

Tane closed warm hands around her hips and lifted her above his head.

Pip thought that should be impossible without forcing him under water, but apparently Tane-who-could-not-be-drowned had plenty of interesting talents.

Super-buoyancy, impressive upper body strength, the ability to talk under water . . . that was all impressive enough, but what *really* impressed her was his ability to impress *her*. It had never been easy to impress tiny Pippin Pearmain. Experts had tried.

After being in contact with so much salt water, she hoped wherever they were going had a cup of camomile tea to offer.

She also hoped her lacy knickers, which she realised she was wearing after all, survived their unusual experience in shape and elastic integrity.

They were labelled *do not bleach* and *do not tumble dry*. There was nothing in the label directive about dunking them in the sea and changing — what? Realities? She didn't quite know.

The sun had come up while they swam, and she was glad of it, as it meant she could make out the vagaries of the path. The rock was uneven, but bare feet made it easy to get a grip.

"Turn right at the fork," Tane said.

Pip immediately wanted to turn left out of perversity.

Maybe he realised that, because he added, "There's a sea-fay man who lairs on the other path, and you might not feel comfortable in his company."

"Not sure I feel comfortable in yours," she retorted.

"That's an untruth, Miss Pearmain."

"A bit, maybe. What are you?"

She recalled Zach's odd expression when she'd asked that about Jisinia. Now she had an inkling of the reason.

She was unsure of exactly where she was, but she knew it wasn't anywhere near Bass Strait.

Another world. Another reality. A right-hand turn from life. Over there . . . it's the land of those old stories.

Tane said, "I'm a jeweller. A silversmith. I'm a husband and a father — and a father-by-love which means whatever we choose. I have parents who are good friends with one another and who love me. I have dear semi-brothers and semi-sisters from my dad and my mammy, and dear sisters-and-brothers-by-love. I have nievies I'm fond of. One day I hope to be a grandfather."

A family man. A seducer — a propositioner — a serial hugger, but also a family man.

"But what *are* you, Tane-who-can't-be-drowned? Besides as slippery as all get out?"

"I told you — Oh, I *see*. You're asking for my order."

"Maybe I am." The cliff path was steep, and she paused to catch her breath.

Tane paused behind her, and she turned and gazed past him and out over the sea. It glimmered with silver and lacy waves, and she saw the island he'd mentioned, blued by distance.

She'd always loved the concept of islands . . . countries in miniature.

The island, the cliffs, and the ocean were almost overwhelmingly beautiful. Pip vaguely remembered climbing a

hill somewhere in Queensland and looking down over an is-
land-studded sea in the dawn light. That had been another
holiday with Big Nanna de Leon who had taken her along
with Lupin and Juniper. Pip tried, and failed, to remember
where Big Pop had been. Was that one of the years he went to
France? It seemed an odd place for him to go. Maybe he was
looking up relatives. Jan might know. He had been in the
navy. Maybe he had friends or relatives there.

This ocean view of *over there* was even better.

"Oh look—a dolphin!" She pointed as a flashing silver-
green figure leaped and twisted above the waves.

More movement caught her attention along the other path.
She saw a tall woman in a cloak leaning out from the cliff,
apparently also watching the dolphin.

The creature leaped again—

Pip froze.

The woman dropped her cloak, standing pale and naked
with strawberry-blonde curls blowing around her shoulders.

In a blink, she had sprung out and down, meeting the
ocean headfirst with barely a splash, then swimming out to
embrace the not-dolphin.

Tane said mildly, "That's the seafay man, Miss Pearmain.
His name's Lore Mor Arlodh. Style him *Master Mor Arlodh* if
you chance to meet him. He will probably insult you, but you
are at liberty to insult him back. He will expect it. If you don't,
he'll feel at liberty to sneer."

"Who was—is she all right?"

"The lady is his wife, Mistress Xanthe. She is perfectly all
right. If he insults you, and if you insult him back, she will
correct him and commend you. They will both enjoy that.
Have you rested enough?"

Pip stared a little longer, then decided she had seen
enough—more than enough—of the seafay and his wife. The
stories in *Grandmother's Sunshine* had never mentioned *that*

sort of behaviour.

"Are *you* a seafay man?" she asked with a twinge of unease.

Tane chuckled. "No. I'm a halfling. I don't have even a drop of salt water blood. Dad is a pisky man and a mutie from Treborrow and Mam is a water maid from the falls. I have water talent from Mam and silver talent from Dad, although I'm not a mutie. Master Mor Arlodh has a far stronger sea-gift than I have, but then, he's a pureblood from the salt."

Pip didn't disbelieve him. Refusing to believe what was in front of her would have been idiotic. "So, you're not human."

"Not even a bit," Tane said cheerfully.

Again, she believed him. His shaggy hair was dry and so was his kilt. No water beaded his skin, and he smelled of apricots and bread.

She, on the other hand, felt damp and draggled and soon to be horribly sticky.

Pip climbed faster. "If you're not human, what the *devil* are you doing playing third crewman on a yacht in Bass Strait with an early childhood teacher and a woman who discusses internal cats and steals phones?"

"I asked myself that yesterday," he mused.

"And what did yourself answer?"

They'd reached the top of the path, and Pip stepped up onto short turf. Gorse bushes bristled nearby, flourishing their coconut-scented blossoms in the gentle air. She glanced down at her feet.

"We'll go the soft way," Tane said. He reached for her hand, and she let him take hold of it. "No harm. I'm not encroaching and I'm not patronising. I just don't want to lose you down a rabbit hole or over the cliff. I'd have to fetch you back, and that would be inconvenient."

Pip cast her gaze around. The air was so clear it almost shone. Her heart did a few glad skips as the world of *Grandmother's Sunshine* bloomed about her.

This place was unbelievable, but so was everything else that had happened since she made that call and spoke to the man called Trip.

Tane moved on slowly, pacing himself to her much shorter strides. He wasn't especially tall, but she had the feeling he usually moved much faster. As they walked, he belatedly answered her question about how he came to be crewing on *Tulpenmanie*.

"When I was younger, Dad's kin-cousin Keeley found Dad's first son—the one he made with a human maid a long time ago. My big brother's name is Jory—and his last name is Pendennis, like mine. My other cousins—Keeley's sons—have a human dad called Drew. They told me a lot about the human realm where they mostly live. I wanted to visit them and see films and go in cars. Dad said *better not,* and Mam said, *Dear one, no,* but I went anyway. Keeley arranged it."

Pip wondered how that had gone down with his parents.

He said, "It was—so hard at first. The air was thick, and the water was dull. People found me odd, I think. Jory and his love, Linda, helped me to fit in and *live human* for a while. I'm sure I was a great nuisance to them, but Jory is my brother and Linda is *Linda.* They never let me feel burdensome. I went to films and learned all sorts of things Mam never imagined. Dad knew them, because he and Drew were going round the markets back then, same as they do now.

"Then after a bit I found forever with my Jillian Jules. I still spend some of my time in your world, because it's Jory's and Linda's and Laura's and Jamie's—and Drew's and—"

Pip felt she was growing cross-eyed. She hoped he wouldn't recite *all* his odd part-human relatives.

"So I sell my jewellery at markets with Dad and Drew. Jillian and I go to the movies sometimes to remember when we met—"

Pip opened her mouth to comment on the peculiarity of

that but shut it again as he continued.

"Jory's Linda is a kind sister-by-love to me. She drives for Vouch-Safe. Jamie drives for them, too, now. Linda said I might want to help with some vouchers, but I don't drive, so Jamie said Zach . . ."

No doubt, Tane went on with his complicated explanation, but Pip lost the connection. The scenery had gone. All she saw now was a blur of blue and mist and green. "What — " she interrupted.

"Nearly there," Tane said. "No, don't let go — "

Pip dragged her hand free of his. She felt a sharp braking sensation, as if she'd jumped from a moving train.

She staggered and promptly fell over, landing in deep grass.

She looked up into a dazzle of blue.

Tane had vanished.

She closed her eyes.

It was just too, too much.

However did I, tiny Pippin Pearmain, ever think an adventure could work for me?

CHAPTER THREE. JANE

Pip lay there for a few seconds, or possibly for a few minutes, until the sun's warmth suddenly ceased to bathe her skin. She opened her eyes and focused on a face peering down at her with an anxious air. It belonged to a girl in her late teens. She had grey eyes and long shiny hair hanging in braids over a blue dress that looked like an ankle-length T-shirt. The braids were woven and bound with silver thread.

"Hello," Pip said, cautiously.

"Greet you," the girl said. Her lips tilted into a delightful smile, and she offered her hand to Pip. "Shall I help you up, mistress?"

Pip took the offered hand and accepted the support. When she gained her feet, she noted the girl's slightly elongated face and slanting eyes.

"My name's Jane," the girl said.

Jane. Really? A fairy is called Jane?

She realised she'd decided to think of this place—this realm—as fairyland until or unless she came to a better understanding.

"Are you Miss Pearmain? If you are, please come with me. Dadda's awfully sorry he lost you. He asked me to find you and bring you to Fosscot. He'd have come back himself, but he thought you might squeal at him or stamp on his toes. He admits he deserves it, and Mam says it's a wonder it doesn't happen more often. Jules offered to stamp on his toes for you if you want, but I don't think he meant it. He was laughing. Not at you, Miss Pearmain. Just at the look on Dadda's face when he confessed to losing you."

Pip said, "Is it far?"

"Not far at all. We can *go*, or we can walk. What would you like to do?"

"What do you mean—go?"

Jane pursed her lips. "*Go*. Hold hands and hurry-scurry. There in no time."

Ah.

"I think I'd rather walk."

"I like to walk," Jane said, stepping out then slowing back to match with Pip. She added, "Dadda said he carried you off from a boat *over there*. Mam's scolding him. She doesn't think it's quite as funny as Jules does. Dadda never thinks before he acts—that's the water blood for you. Mind, Mama Tam is water through and through, and *she* makes plans. Uncle Jory says she's a *long-range* planner."

"That explains a few things," Pip said, though it didn't explain them very clearly.

Jane said sweetly, "Miss Pearmain, you look a bit damp and crumpled and raggedy. Would you like to have a comb and a dry shift like mine? I have one with camomile daisies around the hem. You'd look lovely in it, and we could hitch it up with a belt since you're not very big. I could get it now, or we could go into the fossmere to get the salt off you first."

Pip remembered Tane had mentioned skinny dipping.

"I would like to change, but it would be better to wash first. I don't want to make one of your dresses all salty." She frowned, suddenly. "Jane, do you know what time it is?"

"Past sun-up," Jane said obligingly.

"I know, but the *time*."

"Oh! Clock time, you mean." She looked up at the sky. "I should think it's a few minutes to seven. Dadda got home at twenty-to, and he had to explain, then it took me a little while to find you."

Seven!

"I have to do my ballet practice at seven."

Jane's face bloomed into another charming smile. "Me too! Laura—that's my dear cousin—Uncle Jory's daughter—is teaching me and she said I was to practise *faithfully* if I want to dance with the *Forevers*. Richie does. She's Uncle Jory's sister and she's *beautiful*. Come on, let's *go*. Then we can do our practice together, *then* we can dip in the fossmere, and I can make you feel special in my camomile dress." She put out her hand and caught Pip's, the way Tane had done.

The scenery blurred again.

This time, Pip held on.

"Slow time now," Jane said after a short while. "Count down ten, nine . . ."

Pip counted down and on *zero*, they stopped.

She didn't fall this time.

"Jane, you're much more explainable than your father," she said. She paused. "Or maybe I mean *explanatory*. Yes, I think that's the word."

Jane giggled. "That's what Mam says. That's why she sent *me* and not Sulane or Trae. Sulane is learned, but she sometimes jumps bits of explanations." She pointed out to the side. "There's Fosscot, where we live. The fossmere is just through the trees, and *there* is the place I do my dancing practice. See? Trae is waiting to play for us."

Pip looked from the large, whitewashed cottage to the tangle of autumn-leaved trees then to a flat shelf of chalk. A boy of about twelve, wearing a kilt like Tane's, sat on a boulder, swinging his legs and eating figs from a blue bowl.

Jane led Pip over to the chalk stage. She indicated a pair of trestles with a narrow pole clamped between them.

"That's the barre. Jamie made it for me. He's Laura's brother . . . he's lovely, and so's his mutie dog." She turned to the boy. "Trae, are you ready?"

The boy licked his fingers and pulled a wooden flute from

the belt of his kilt. "You found Dadda's lost lady, then, Janie."

"Yes, and she *dances*! Isn't that a treat? Oh! Miss Pearmain, this is my brother, Trae. He threw piskywards, so he tends to be annoying, but he plays for me every morning and he never complains."

The boy, who looked altogether less reliable than Jane, grinned at Pip. "Hugs to you, Miss Pearmain. I *am* very annoying, but that's all right. Dadda is, too." He lifted the flute to his lips and played a sweet trill before slipping into a piece Pip recognised as one she'd heard years ago during a film shoot.

She realised with a shock that it was the one Alain Barfleur had played on his lute during the long breaks in filming *The House of Heriot* . . . the ones where they'd been stuck in the green room while it rained. She'd loved it then, but she'd never heard it again once the shooting wrapped. She'd tried to find it in music libraries, but without a title, a composer or an artist, she'd had no luck.

"Oh, what's the name of that—"

She broke off because Jane had run gracefully over to the makeshift barre and was limbering up. She was barefoot, and so was Pip.

This might be . . . interesting.

Pip joined her at a more sedate pace and moved into pliés.

I'll ask about the tune later.

It was decidedly odd to dance barefoot on chalk with a graceful teenaged girl working alongside and a kilted boy playing the flute as accompaniment, but the comfort of not having missed her morning practice flowed over her like honey.

I'm so dedicated . . . ha! Oops . . . She'd stubbed her toe as the universe took revenge on her mental boasting.

The air was pure, and a soft breeze began to dry her sticky long T-shirt and lifted her hair from her perspiring neck.

She glanced at Jane, who performed her exercises with

determined concentration. Evidently, the girl hadn't been learning long enough for the exercises to live in muscle memory. She had natural fluidity, though — far more than Pip had ever had.

Should she exercise in good form for the entire hour? Or should she do her usual mix of exercises interspersed with free dancing?

Desire won over duty.

Who cared how she employed her practice time? It was years since she'd been required to dance on stage or in a film. If she lived long enough to become the dancing centenarian she had suggested to Jan and Lupin at the Delmsford Flower Show, she could still make her fortune. Wasn't there an old adage about a dog walking on its hind legs . . . not surprising that it did it well, but astonishing that it did it at all?

Besides, if she exercised in good form, the way she *didn't* do at home, she'd be showing off. That might earn her another stubbed toe.

She performed her final set of sautés — a term that always made her think of onions and butter in a pan — and moved away from the barre. The boy's tune faltered, and Jane paused in a demi plié.

"Sorry," Pip said.

Trae took the chance to consume another fig. "Have you finished?" he mumbled through a mouthful.

"It's not the full hour," Jane said. She smiled at Pip. "Do you not do a full hour, Miss Pearmain? It's absolutely fine if you don't. Laura says we all have to find our own rhythm. Overtraining is no better than not training."

"I do an hour, but I don't spend it all in exercises. I like to dance, and your brother's music is far better than what I use at home."

Jane's eyes lit up. She *was* an expressive girl. She clasped her hands under her chin in a way that would have looked affected if she'd been a human teenager. "Laura says dance is as much about expressing the soul as it is about technique. Richie—that's Dadda's semi-sister and Uncle Jory's whole one, who dances with *Forever*, has *so* much soul in her dancing. Shall we do some of that?"

"If it suits you." Pip was unused to sharing her dance practice and she realised it might have become an obsessive habit rather than the active delight it had once been.

Trae swallowed his fig and said, "Does that mean I can play free?"

"Yes! It's such good practice to adapt to the unexpected. Ready, Miss Pearmain?"

Pip indicated that she was.

Trae raised the flute again and played a swinging tune that sounded like a nursery rhyme, although not one Pip knew. It suggested a set of plies then bounded off into a skipping rhythm before segueing into another tune.

Trae played on, bouncing from tune to tune, some slow, and some fast.

Pip was familiar with some of them, but others were new to her.

She composed chains in her mind as she danced, relishing the extra room and lack of furniture to avoid. Lemonwood Cottage was cosy rather than spacious, but here on the chalk stage she had all the room she needed and no censorious cats suggesting she'd be better employed by running along to the shop to buy more cheese.

After a while, Trae eased into a gentle repetitive refrain and Jane began bends and rises, stretching her limbs and flexing her shoulders and wrists.

The cool down.

Pip followed suit. She felt hot and breathless, and her throat was parched.

Time for my lemon and water . . . oh. I'll have to miss my date with the lemon tree . . . Should have gone to that island with the lemon tree and the bucket instead of coming here. Oh, wait . . . that one must be back near *Tulpenmanie*. And if I'd not come here I'd have missed dancing with Jane.

Despite her thirst, she felt *good.*

The old girl's still got it.

She waited for the universe to swat her, but evidently one toe stub had been enough.

Chapter Four. Fossmere

Trae let the music trickle to a halt. Without delay, he slid down from his boulder and came across to Pip. "I think that's enough for you, Miss Pearmain. It was fun. You look a bit hot, so get Jane to take you to the fossmere. Mam will give you something to drink. What do you like?"

"Lemon and water or camomile tea," Pip said.

"That's easy. Janie?"

"That sounds wonderful. Can you—"

He grinned. "I'll try not to tip it over your head."

Jane was perspiring, but she contrived to look dewy rather than sticky.

Pip felt an unaccustomed giggle rising in her chest. Tane's children were chips off the old block indeed. Jane would delight the eye dressed in a black plastic rubbish bag, and Trae was already a practised charmer of older ladies.

"How many of you are there?" she asked Jane as Trae sauntered off towards the cottage.

"Well, Dadda and Mam, then me—then there's Sulane and Trae, and Mirri and Tallien—he's the newest babby. There's Sam, but she doesn't live with us. She's Jules', and she has a little'un of her own . . . Soash. She and her forever come to visit often, and Sam plays along with Trae—she's the only one of us with enough music to give him a stretch. Mam says Trae needs not to be sitting on his laurels, whatever that means." Jane blew out her cheeks. "Sometimes Sam's friends from the tower come, but I won't tell you too many names. I don't expect you know them. Then there's my own Ardal—I expect

25

you'll meet him soon." She held out her hand. "Come along to the fossmere and we can skinny dip — er — if that's all right with you?" She looked worried.

Pip considered her options. She could be middle-aged and stuffy and *human,* or she could set this nice child's mind at rest. After all, she had lived through the 1970s when anything went.

"That's okay with me, as long as you don't mind a few wrinkles and floppy or knobbly bits."

Jane relaxed. "Mama Tam — that's my granny — has those and she's *beautiful.*"

"Is she your dad's mother or your mum's?"

"Dadda is her eldest. Mam's mother is Nanna Zena. She's lovely too, and she's older than Mama Tam. She lives in Brisbane, *over there.* I'm going to stay with her for a little while when Jules arranges it with her. She's human, like you — mostly."

Well — maybe Tane's Jillian won't be a challenge after all if she's human like her mum.

But that was false thinking. Even if Jillian was human, why should she not be a challenge? Humans must be one of the most challenging species around.

"What was the name of that tune?" Pip asked.

"Um?" Jane seemed confused.

Pip hummed a few bars of it . . . not in her high-pitched *considering* hum that had so annoyed Lupin, but in a lower and more musical register.

Jane said, "That one's called "Silk and Circumstance". It's such a sweet tune, and it's perfectly paced for dancing. It's the one the courtfolk play to start their balls. Ardal told me. He has a courtfolk friend who trains horses too, and *he* is friends with a hob maid named Bluebell who goes to the overflow dances — "

Jane's explanation seemed likely to go on until dinnertime, so Pip tuned it out for a wee while then broke into a pause to

say, "Who wrote it — who recorded it — er — *do* you have re-
cordings?"

"We don't, but I understand what you mean," Jane said after a blinking moment during which she must have recalled
how the conversation began. "Laura and Richie . . . oh, and
Ammie — she's Laura's aunt — they sometimes sing together at
festivals and Laura played me a recording called *Magic Fiddle*
when I went to visit Uncle Jory's family. "Silk and Circumstance" was one of the pieces."

"So — who recorded it?"

"It was a fiddler — Tamzin Campania — Laura said it was a
big thing because *no* one usually records courtfolk music."

"Oh. I thought it might have been a lutist I knew once."

"Do you mean Court Leopold? He plays the lute and he's
friends with Mistress Campania. I don't think he'd play "Silk
and Circumstance," though — he composes his own tunes."

"No — this one's name was Alain Barfleur."

Jane shook her head regretfully. "Sorry, I don't know him.
But then, we don't know many courtfolk. They don't usually
mix with waterfolk *or* piskies. I *do* know Master Leopold, because his wife is my best friend Liffey's good friend — she's
wed to Uncle Finn Rivers, Dadda's semi-brother. Liffey is
wed to him, I mean."

Pip stopped walking.

"I'm *so* sorry," Jane said in her sweet tone. "I'm doing what
I vowed I wouldn't do, talking and talking until you must be
ready to put your hands over your ears. Jules says I explain
too much sometimes."

Pip reflected that she still had no idea who Jules was. Jane
had mentioned him a few timed, but there was no way in the
world that Pip would ever ask for clarification. Jane would be
bound to tell her in tortuous detail.

At least she had the name for that long-sought tune.

Silk and Circumstance.

It was the perfect name, and now she knew it, she might

find the recording Jane mentioned. *Magic Fiddle,* by Tamzin Campania. She'd remember that artist's name. It sounded delightful, and hauntingly familiar-by-association. One of her favourite childhood books had a protagonist named *Tamzin,* and *Campania* was the name of a Tasmanian town where she had holidayed with Big Nanna de Leon and Lupin and Jan. Big Nanna had taken two holidays a year, spending a week in a place she hadn't been before. She'd taken Pip and her cousins as soon as they were old enough to travel without fuss. Pip remembered Jack Kelly Lake, Campania, the place in Queensland, and of course, Jellico Bay, and a camping trip to Nugget Creek where they'd poked around the old gold mine.

When did that stop? Was it when Lupin went to university?

Pip couldn't remember. She realised she'd just accepted Big Nanna's holidaying habits, but now she came to think of it, they must have been somewhat peculiar. Why on Earth had she chosen to go to Jack Kelly Lake, or to Jellico Bay, or to Campania, or to that Queensland town, or to Gilchrist in New South Wales? Jan might know.

Despite her apology, Jane kept chatting away gently as they walked on towards the shaggy tangle of autumn trees and Pip pondered matters past.

A narrow path led through the trees, winding just because it could. The scents of fallen leaves mixed with the sweetness of late flowers and nuts and acorns lay scattered in the leaf mould. Pip wanted to look about but, mindful of her bare feet, she kept her attention on the path.

Thus, she missed the first sight of what Jane referred to as the fossmere.

The first she noted of it was the sound of pouring water and the giggles of little children.

She looked up and caught her breath.

She reflected that she should have known what to expect. *Foss* was a dialect word meaning, among other things, waterfall, and *mere* was a pool or a lake. Jane's fossmere was a bewitching combination of both, with water pouring from the lip of a limestone overhang tossing rainbows over the natural basin. The rock wall, alive with ferns, dipped in to form a cave, and the limestone had made miniature plunges and cups for those not wanting to swim in the bubbling water.

Logs, or possibly branches, formed hand-holds or places to rest.

Several people were there already. Tane stood chest-deep in the water, arguing with a vociferous child of around four years old who kept dipping under the water. A girl of fourteen or so sat in one of the plunges with a laughing baby in her lap, and two women stood under the fall itself, apparently unfazed by the beat of water on their heads and faces. One was a blonde who looked like Jane and so was presumably Jillian, and the other an older woman with a serene expression and long grey hair caught in a loose bun. It should have been soggy and clinging, but it looked almost dry.

"That's Mama Tam," Jane said cheerfully. "Isn't she lovely? Oh—and there's Uncle Finn and darling Liffey! I haven't seen her for ages!" She ran ahead and stripped off her long dress before plunging into the water and hugging a slender redhead who hugged her back with obvious affection. Alone among the women she had clothing—a brief green camisole.

Pip approached more slowly, feeling increasingly uncertain. She'd agreed to a dip with a young woman who had gone out of her way to put her at ease. She hadn't expected a mixed crowd.

Jane and the red-haired girl had their heads together in the manner of good friends everywhere, leaving the girl's male companion to notice Pip.

His gaze fixed on her, and he looked startled, then enchanted.

A sudden lull in the conversation let his voice ring out

clearly above the beat of the foss.

"Darlin' Liffey, here's a wee one chin high for you!"

The redhead turned a startled face in his direction. "Finn, ye spalpeen! What a thing to say! Sure I'll tweak ye for that if the maid doesn't do it herself."

Pip gulped. The words were all right. She *was* small—it was her stock in trade. However, the young man, with his beguiling Irish accent, was startling in more than one way. He was decently waist-deep in the water, but there was a good deal of skin on display, and what skin! Tane had a sun-kissed glow, Trae and Jane were human-normal, but this one was *green*.

Chapter Five. Mama Tam

Pip usually prided herself on keeping a steady demeanour. In her quiet decade at Jellico Bay she'd gone days without more than pleasantries exchanged with Wanda at Jelly-and-Juice when she picked up her weekly order of cakes and tarts, or a companionable hour of tea and biscuits with Mister Clancy.

She and Mister Clancy had been friends for ten years, but she'd never known his first name until after his recent passing when she'd gone to his funeral, then to the estate auction. She'd purchased a wooden wishing well and what she had dubbed the Clancy Bucket. Jan had that bucket now.

Mister Clancy's death had been a bit of a shock, as he'd not been ill. He'd eaten a tart instead of his usual Bushman's Best Biscuit, but that was perfectly understandable. Faced with a choice, Pip would have taken the tart as well. She usually did. It was only since his passing that she'd started eating Bushman's Best, and that was just because she didn't want to waste them.

Mister Clancy also, according to the eulogy given by an old priest she didn't know, had been very much older than she'd thought.

Donovan Clancy might have been a bit deaf, or possibly inattentive, but he'd had all his teeth and a goodly thatch of iron-grey hair. She'd liked him. She'd miss their conversations.

She often listened in to conversations at the post office or the supermarket, but most of her own dialogues had been with the original cat. She spoke to him just as she'd speak to any sentient companion . . . although he *very* occasionally seemed to read her mind . . . and he and his apprentice the back-up cat responded in clear Cat-Morse. At first it had been only the original cat, whose name was probably Kittisack, but lately the back-up, the delightful Amberjill, had joined the conversation. Even more lately the third cat, who happened to be made of pottery and decorated with painted flowers, had shown proficiency in Cat-Morse too.

Even now, in the magical land of *over there,* Pip was unsure how those exchanges worked, or even *whether* they worked. Perhaps they were pure imagination. Maybe Jane knew.

After her peculiar journey to this place, she should have been more accepting of strangeness, but the sight of this green-skinned young man still startled her.

Having weathered his girlfriend's scolding he looked remorseful, slid down chest deep in the water, and forged towards her.

Before she could react he'd hopped up on the rim of the pool and made an approach with both hands out in supplication.

"I'm that sorry — I niver did know how to hold me tongue." He was a good bit taller than Pip, but he brought his head down level with hers. "Tweak me nose now, an' make it a good one to save darlin' Liffey the trouble. Sure, I'll howl like a banshee to entertain ye for your throuble."

Pip stared at him.

Like his girl, he had some clothing on — in his case, drawstring britches. He had hazel eyes, and his wet hair had a rusty tint to it.

And his skin was the green of olives.

"Fergal McClattery's toenails, Finn, get away from the poor maid!" The redhead's voice had lost its sweet lilt and she sounded like an exasperated parent. She disengaged from

Jane and got up on the bank where she grabbed the young man and gave him a push. "Stand off — you're scaring her to death with all that blarney."

Pip's mouth was drier than ever, but she managed to intervene. "It's okay — I was just startled."

The redhead put an arm around her, and that was startling too. She smelled of clover and hay. "Sure, lovie, ye must be human for all ye're so very wee." The lilt was back in her voice and Pip thought she was trying not to laugh. "I'm Liffey Rosheen," she said. She indicated the green lad. "This one here is my own man, Finn Rivers. To be sure he's green, but not so green as some. It's inborn to him, so the hue won't be rubbing off, and when our babby is born we'll look for no more than a wee bit of colour — none at all should she be a colleen."

Pip said, "I'm Pippin Pearmain," rather faintly.

"To be sure ye are!" Liffey said cordially. "Banshee Mary — an' I niver laughed so much other than seein' ye nip up the mast in *Shamrock Sailors*. 'Tis one o' Aunt Livvie's favourite films."

That's it, Pip thought. I'm hallucinating. Maybe dreaming or possibly gone stark mad.

By now, Jane had got out of the water. "Uncle Finn, it's all right. Just come back in. Get Dadda to explain to you."

"For pity's sake!" Blonde Jillian stepped forward from the cascade and raised her voice above the hubbub. "All of you, get back here — Jane — *Jane* — bring Miss Pearmain to me, then get her a cup of tea. Trae's sent some over not five minutes ago."

Jane looked relieved and held out her hand. "Miss Pearmain, I'm *so* sorry. I just ran off and left you. I'm as bad as Dadda, but I saw darlin' Liffey, and everything went out of my head. Come and talk to Mam and Mama Tam. Camomile tea, wasn't it? I'll pour you some."

What could Pip say to the remorseful Jane but that it was perfectly okay, and that she'd love to talk to the other women? Mama Tam looked around her age, at least.

Though she wasn't so sure of that waterfall.

To her relief, the elder of the two women came out and indicated one of the natural rock scoops.

"Mistress, do come over here with me. The younglings are so unrestful." She smiled and her eyes crinkled, suggesting a bit of unrestfulness was fine by her.

Pip saw immediately where Jane got her sweetness of nature. Mama Tam reminded her of Little Mum and Little Nannas Laurel and Pearmain. Tears suddenly lapped her eyelids.

She slid obediently into the scoop and settled on a shelf, leaving her chest-deep.

Tam said, "Maybe take off that, and souse it well. I'll dry it for you, after." She indicated the T-shirt.

Pip stripped it off. She was sure no one in this company would care if she went topless, bottomless or hung from her heels.

Tam slipped in beside her and took possession of the shirt. She rubbed it through her hands, wrung it, shook it out and flipped it over one of the logs. "All done," she said, and Pip watched as dry patches formed over the cloth.

Magic, she thought, but she just said, "Can you do my knickers?"

Tam said, serenely, "I can, my love. I do my man's drawers all the time." Her face creased in a grin. "Be sure he *will* wear them, to be *dacent* as he says, though I tell him it's a great waste of time."

Pip looked about but saw no one likely to be this woman's husband.

Tam said, "He's not here, lovie. He's off in the village having a crack with what Jules calls *Team Tam*." She nodded towards Finn. "There you see one of the sons he made with me.

We made two more, too!" She looked fondly on the young man. "A dear lad and helpful, but his tongue runs on like his da's . . . and mine." A sideways nod indicated Tane. "My eldest — made him with the most beautiful pisky man I ever saw — the nicest, too."

Pip noted that Tam was almost as talkative as Jane. "Do you have other children, Miss . . . Missus . . ."

"Just Tam, lovie. And yes! I have Whim and Becca, my sweet maids. Made 'em with William Cliff and Moss the beechmaster." She smiled. "That's a handful more babbies than most of my order bears, and if it had been up to me there would have been another from a handsome human man. I picked him out especially, but he said no. Too late now. Never mind — got the grandbabies to make me smile. Five from Tane and Jillie, and dear Sam, of course from Jules, and little Soash . . . then Whim and Becca have two apiece and Finn's Liffey will soon be swelling. Rye and Lee are waiting a while — to see how it's done, they say." She chuckled.

"Jane's a lovely girl," Pip ventured. A small lump seemed to settle in her heart.

"All our children are lovely — made in love and friendliness, you see," Tam said. She added, "Who have you to love, mistress?"

Pip opened her mouth to say she had no one, but Tam looked at her expectantly and she didn't want to disappoint.

"I live with three cats," she admitted.

Tam nodded in approval. "Then you have plenty of love in your life."

"They don't exactly snuggle up and purr," Pip protested. "Two of them not often and one of them not at all."

"That's not what you want anyway. You want companions with their own minds. Tell me about them."

Pip told her. She supposed the splashing and chatter continued, but she ceased to be aware of it. Once she realised this, she understood this gentle woman was very different from herself . . . and from anyone she knew.

Tam listened with visible glee to anecdotes about the original cat and the back-up cat and their determination to have cheese, and their penchant for vanishing if strangers appeared. She also seemed to enjoy the tale of Lupin's cat.

"You don't seem surprised," Pip said with suspicion.

Tam said, "I'm not. I heard this tale—or part of it—from a dear friend who comes to visit me sometimes."

"Who do you know who could possibly know my business? Or Jan and Lupin's . . ."

"Her name's Beatrice. I wouldn't say she'd had as many men as I have, but she wed all four of the ones that did fall under her approval. I wed just the one, so perhaps we're equal. Her name these days is Beattie Inkersoll, for she wed the old red cat after his life-love passed to glory. She says they'll wear out together, and I wish her a long life for that."

What?

Pip's head spun. A *cat?*

"He's not always a cat—just now and again. Beattie says it's restful to have him snuggle in her lap at times. She's no mutie herself, but she comes from that stock. Rory's a listener, a guardian, they say. A fine man—though I never got to have him." She shrugged. "It would have been nice, but not the right thing for him, he always said."

"Who says he's a guardian?" Pip blurted. Hearing of Tam's love life, tabulated with such good cheer, made her feel peculiar.

Tam said, "The fay cats hereabouts think highly of him. He holds the hands of folk who are off to glory and lays on blessings to speed them with a smile."

Unbelievable as all this sounded, something twinged in Pip's mind.

Lupin's cat had said something about Lupin having her hand held as she died. And the cats . . . *her* cats . . . had definitely Cat-Morsed approval of a guardian.

"What exactly are fay cats?" she asked.

Tam considered, drawing idle patterns in the water. It responded to her hand by holding the designs for a few seconds more than water should.

"The cats that live hereabouts . . . and a few of them go *over there*. I can't say what other cats look like, sweet. I don't go through the gates. My kind can't."

"Your son does."

"Tane—yes. He *would* go when he was younger, for all his dad and I told him *no*. He said he'd be fine as spring rain. Turned out he was half right. He *can* live there but he does better here. And he's the only one of my children who does it at all. Finn and his brothers can't *pass* any more than their dad and I can, and the maids—Whim could, but Becca couldn't, so neither of them do—not so far. Tane offered to take them in hand, but they thanked him kindly and declined." She laughed. "Just as well, maybe. You can't pretend you didn't get a big surprise when you saw my lad Finn."

"He is rather striking," Pip admitted.

"His da is, too." Tam rolled her eyes. "Oh, the trouble that man gave me! A beautiful green babby was all I was asking for, but would he give one to me? It was thank-ye, but no, and *no*, and *niver* . . . and waving a ring at me and cooking me tatties and greens—and kissing me with his blarneying eyes until I said *yes*. After that I got my green way babby and two more besides."

"That sounds as if you were collecting different babies," Pip ventured.

"So I was. My folk thought it was odd of me, but after I made Tane with the finest pisky man in Treborrow, I got a notion for more. There were so many fine men, and I chose the best for my babbies." She leaned back. "Since Beattie wed the old red cat, we call kin with him through Tane—Beattie being blood-bound to that fine pisky man."

"Does this old cat ever come to where I live?" Pip asked, sidestepping all the complications.

"Oh, he's back and forth and in and out. Beattie too—and her friend Sofia. But tell me more about you . . ."

"My life's not as full of family as yours," Pip said, but she told Tam about the bucket list, the sly-eyed gooseberry and the sentient lemon.

Tam seemed entertained, but after a while, she reached for Pip's hand and examined the tektite ring.

"My Tane used his talent on this."

"Yes, he resized it for me. It's never fitted before."

"See mine." Tam displayed her hand with its band of red gold, ornamented with a tiny green stone. "I wasn't sure about accepting it, but Liam said *ring first, then babby*. I thought, well, I'll get my babby. Then if the ring weighs too hard on me, I'll take the ring off and leave it with Liam, lift the tiddler from his cradle, and head home to the falls."

"You didn't, though," Pip said.

"I did not. Maybe I would have, but Liam came to me after Finn was born, and he opened the door to his cottage.

"I asked why, and he said, so long as this door stands un-latched, ye're free to leave, lovie. All I ask is that ye often bring me son to see me so we'll niver be strangers. And maybe lie with me once in a while." She shrugged, and added, "Then he bound up the latch so it couldn't fall closed accidentally. And so I'll stay forever."

Chapter Six. Skinny Dipping

Pip puffed out her cheeks. Tam's romance sounded like something from a fairy tale.

Tam went on holding her hand. Pip looked down to see her skin wrinkling into pale prune waves from prolonged immersion. Tam's hand might have been dipped in the water just a second ago. She looked up at her shirt and knickers over the log, dry and clean and even unwrinkled.

"Can you do that to my hands?" she asked, indicating the pristine garments with her free one.

Tam lifted their joined hands out of the water. The water slid off like mercury from a spoon and she stroked Pip's fingers back to normality.

While they'd been conversing, the others had got out of the fossmere. They had arranged themselves on the grass where they sat in a cosy group. Jillian, clad in a long, loose gown, poured tea from a giant pot into assorted cups. Pip was briefly reminded of the three mismatched cups, lily, rose, and iris, which she and her cousins had used at their afternoon tea at the Delmsford Flower Show.

The scene somehow put Pip in mind of a painting she'd seen—people in romantic-era costumes seated on the grass serving tea from a floral pot while others were in the water. It was one of the early Australian impressionists, she thought. C. Miles Brady, maybe, who had painted for a few years then simply stopped. Pip had seen some of his work in a gallery while filming *The Girl in the Frame* back in 2011. She'd picked up a catalogue of the exhibition, but there had been frustratingly little information and the prices on the paintings were beyond her means.

She smelled flowers and figs, and the tantalising scent of her favourite tea.

Jillian lifted a cup in her direction, raising her brows.

"In a bit," Pip mouthed.

She saw Tane, back in his kilt, sprawled with the baby on his chest and the older child snuggled under his arm, possibly asleep.

"I'd like to swim a bit," she said to Tam. "I want to get the salt out of my hair."

"Take your time," Tam said.

Pip said, "When Tane jumped into the sea with me, he gave me some air so I could go under water."

"And you'd like to do that again?"

"Could you do it for me? I don't want to disturb the baby."

Tam reached out to draw Pip into a hug. "Ever kissed a maid before, mistress?"

Pip said, "Of course!" She'd done it for work when she'd played Myra in *Path Untaken*. It hadn't been a problem. She added, gently, "But this isn't going to be *that* sort of kissing."

Tam chuckled, unoffended. "It could be, if you'd wanted, but it can also be just the water-gift."

Tam was warm and soft, and she smelled of wallflowers. Pip received her gift of air, kissed Tam's cheek in gratitude and friendship, and slid out of the shaped stone scoop and into the main pool.

She swam a little way through the dimpled water before she dived under, breathing out slowly as Tane had instructed back in the sea.

She let herself sink, feeling the cool caress of the ripples. Down she went to the floor of the fossmere, where grey-gold pebbles rocked gently with the beat of the water. In some places, ridges of smooth mudstone rose, and she used these to pull herself along, right under the cascade.

When she sensed she was well behind, she came up slowly, to float, spread like a starfish, in the dim cave behind the falls.

There were glow worms and ghostly ferns, and the scent of autumn.

It was noisy in its way with the perpetual pouring of water, but Pip felt a beautiful silence.

She wondered if anyone at home would believe her story if she chose to tell it.

Lupin probably would have. She'd worked for Vouch-Safe and must have met some interesting people. She might have met some of these interesting people, even.

Too late to ask her now.

The cats would believe, of course . . . and now she knew what they were! Fay cats—ha! *Cat-Morse* indeed. The artful things had been playing her from the start. Pip resolved to subject those slippery charmers to an in-depth inquisition when she got home.

Cheese might be withheld to prompt swift and total compliance—though that wouldn't work on Lupin's cat.

Charmed by a guardian.

Had Lupin had any idea what she was making?

The desire for camomile tea was growing, but so was her desire to enjoy this experience. She floated, naked as a baby, watching the glow-worms wink. In their gentle light she saw pockets of different colour in the rock.

After a while, she rolled over and swam cautiously towards the rear wall. She'd just touch that, like a swimmer touching before a tumble turn, or a runner shortening stride to negotiate that orange witches' hat that marked the turnaround.

She swam on.

Surely she should have reached the back wall by now.

She half expected someone, possibly Jane, to come to check on her. No one came.

Pip was glad. Skinny dipping alone in a magical place was an experience she'd never forget.

It was silent when she finally touched the wall, and in the dark, she paused, breathing evenly.

I'm happy. It was a thought that seldom came to her. She was rarely unhappy, she supposed, but here she was, experiencing perfect joy.

She had a desire to leave something of herself behind but what was there? She was naked and her messenger bag, her lifeline, was back on *Tulpenmanie.*

She flattened her hands against the wall, and her fingers hooked into a natural niche.

Right. Pip slid off the heaven and earth ring. She trod water for a while, holding it in her palm.

Is this an impulse? Will I regret leaving it behind now that I can finally wear it?

She thought earnestly of that, and of the reverse situation.

Then she kissed the ring, in gratitude for all the benefits her association with Sully had brought her. It was precious and mysterious. The silver had been mined from the darkness of the earth, and the tektite had fallen from the darkness of space.

It had been Sully's for a time, and hers for longer.

Pip located the niche again and put the ring gently inside.

She lingered a while, feeling her heartbeat and the pleasure of knowing that a little piece of her life would stay behind in this place of fun and family.

It could be her point of contact — the physical thing that bound her to the fossmere.

She turned and swam slowly back towards the falls.

CHAPTER SEVEN. TRANSFORMATION SCENE

The water gift from Tam had probably worn out by now, and Pip emerged from the cavern and trod water again while she watched the heavy mane of the falls pouring ceaselessly into the fossmere.

Probably she could call out and someone would rescue her, but she could also dive or simply step through.

Tam and Jillian had been standing under the full force of the water when she'd arrived with Jane.

She held onto a handy knob of rock and let her feet drop. She was much shorter than Jillian, but Tam was small.

Her toes brushed the smooth rock and pebbles, and she released some air from her lungs to hover before she came to rest on tiptoe.

I can do this.

Cautiously, she released her hold on the stone and stepped forward, almost weightless. The swirl of the water pressed her back.

Diving it must be.

I don't dive.

Yes you do.

Could it possibly be Kittisack sending Cat-Morse from Lemonwood Cottage?

Okay, yes I do. At home, I don't, but here, I do.

Pip counted herself down the way Jane had counted when they were about to drop back to ordinary walking.

When she reached *one,* she drew in a breath and ducked under the water.

The falls pounded around her, but as she surfaced, the water pushed her away into the middle of the fossmere.

Pip wiped water from her eyes and looked up in triumph.

The family on the bank was drinking tea. Jane was bent over, cutting slices from a round brown loaf and passing them to red-haired Liffey, who slathered them with butter.

Tane had woken up—if he'd ever been asleep—and Trae had arrived. He was entertaining the baby with his flute. Tam sat cross-legged talking to her green-skinned son and cuddling Jane's two sisters, one of whom was taller than she was. Two slender women in tunics had joined the party with a toddler who spotted Pip and reached out her arms.

A lanky man, who was possibly forty, sat with his arm around Tane, gazing at the new arrivals with evident affection.

Jillian wasn't there.

All this stamped itself like a photocopy in Pip's mind.

The scene moved like a kaleidoscope, and she glimpsed a bigger picture.

These people were a loving family—some members must be missing—four of Tam's children, her husband and Jamie the driver . . . oh, and his parents and—the links went on like those dances where folk caught hands and moved ever onwards, bringing more people into the dance.

How can this family be so big when the Pearmains, Laurels and de Leons are reduced to three living members?

Pip's happiness rocked on its heels.

The little girls, Tane's youngest daughter and the one belonging to the newcomers, darted away from their custodians, clasped hands and leaped into the water.

They came up, hugging Pip, looking up at her with wide and beautiful eyes.

She swallowed the lump in her throat.

"Hello, my lovelies . . . I'm Pippin."

"My name is Mirri," Tane's daughter said.

"Soash," the toddler said in a softer voice, making the name two syllables.

They grabbed a hand each, drawing Pip towards the edge of the fossmere. "Mistress Pippin . . ."

" . . . Would you like to dance?"

"Trae will play for us . . ."

Pip was almost never self-conscious, but she doubted she was up to dancing naked in this company. It would feel like showing off . . . or something.

"Jane has a shift for you and Mama Tam will help your hair," Mirri stated.

One of the slim women came to kneel on the rim of the fossmere. "Out, you two," she said to the little girls.

They scrambled out and retreated to where the other woman waited.

"My name's Sam," the kneeling woman said. She grinned at Pip. "Don't look so startled. You'll soon get used to this mob." She waved a hand at the company. "I understand your head is probably revolving at great speed."

"It is a bit," Pip admitted.

Sam said, "My mother's — um — part human. She thought she was fully human, but just not normal, for years. So did I. We don't see one another much. Dad's a rainbow of possibilities . . . with a mostly human mother — only just got to know him recently." She jerked her head sideways. "That's him snuggling up to Tane. Yes, they *are,* and yes, they *do,* but I'm not one to judge. Not with my gorgeous Oash to snuggle me." She turned and gave a little wave to the other woman, who had curly hair and a cherubic expression. "I love Oash, and I don't share. Just putting it out there."

"I wasn't about to ask for her," Pip said.

"No . . . well, sorry. I'm a bit possessive. I see Jane's got you a nice dress to put on, so I'll give you a hand out." She turned again and called over her shoulder, "Oash, love, can you send me a towel for Mistress Pip?"

Her—what? Friend with benefits? Wife? Lover? Girl-friend? Whatever she was, she tossed a green beach towel a surprising distance to Sam.

Sam caught it and held it outstretched. "Come on . . ."

Pip scrambled out of the water into the warm embrace of the towel. She was instantly transported to childhood, when Little Mum and the nannas used to receive her out of the bath into their towelling embrace. Sam was *much* taller than any of them except perhaps for Big Nanna de Leon.

"Where do you live?" she asked, as she stepped back from Sam and began to dry herself.

"We live in the pixie forest. Now and again, we go through to the tower, but Oash can't handle the human realm for long. Not sure about Soash, yet. I had a pied-à-terre at the tower for a while, but mostly I stay here . . . aside from the odd festival. I might be going to one quite soon, in fact. We're *hoping* Oash and Soash might be able to come because it's close to a gate-way."

Pip nodded, bending to dry her hair.

"Mama Tam will braid that for you if you like," Sam said.

Jane came up with a wheat-coloured dress with daisies decorating the hem, and she and Sam, working in concert, got it onto Pip with the ease of theatrical dressers.

Mama Tam, now wearing a blue sarong with water lilies splashed across it, glided up and gathered Pip's hair into her hands, singing under her breath. The dripping locks magi-cally dried to just damp, and Tam's clever fingers wove a loose braid.

Jane stepped back and clasped her hands. "Miss Pearmain, you look *so beautiful.*"

Pip thought she probably did—but it was all down to these

lovely women.

Someone—she thought it was Jane's sister Sulane— handed her a cup of tea and a piece of bread and butter spread with honey.

"Dance?" Mirri was at her elbow, persistent as a wasp.

"Miss Pearmain is hungry and thirsty," Jane said.

Pip smiled down at the child. "Give me a few minutes, then we can dance."

Mirri clapped her hands.

Tane called across, "Watch out for that one, lovie . . . she's tricky."

Just like her daddy, then.

Pip took a bite out of the best bread she'd ever had and sipped her tea. Then she walked over to Tane and his companion.

"You finally got your tea then," the other man said, laughing. "I was going to give it to you, but somehow you got hijacked by my mother-by-love. Much nicer term than mother-in-law, don't you think?"

Pip looked at him warily. Surely he hadn't been there when she swam under the foss.

Must have come with Sam and her girlfriend.

Tane laughed. "Jules, stop bewildering poor Miss Pearmain."

The man—Jules—gave her an apologetic grin. "Sorry. I expect you don't know whether you're Arthur or Martha. Sometimes, neither do I."

Tane said, "Well, my love, I do, and that's what matters."

Pip said, suspiciously, "What have you done with Jillian?"

Jules' face lit up in an evil grin. "This is where I say, *Miss Pearmain, I am your father,* with suitable *dum-dum-dum* sound-effects. Actually, I'm Sam's father, and Oash's, in the by-love fashion, but I'm also—"

The baby, who had gone to sleep in Tane's lap after Trae went off to get bread, suddenly woke, screwed up his face and wailed. Jules sighed, lifting his free hand to his chest. "Best hand him over," he said.

Tane kissed the squalling baby and passed him to Jules, who tugged open his shirt, shimmered, and morphed into Jillian.

Pip squawked nearly as loudly as the baby.

Chapter Eight. Lord What Fools

Pip spent the night at Fosscot, bedded down in the wide combination kitchen in a kind of nest stuffed with something Jane referred to as springyweed.

She woke in the night when the baby wailed.

Jillian emerged into the kitchen and sat in a rocking chair to feed him.

Pip looked at her doubtfully in the faint light emanating from a lantern. She'd discovered there was no electricity at Fosscot.

Jillian said, "Are you awake, Pip?"

"Yes."

"I expect Tally woke you. He's the *loudest* baby we've managed so far. The others would wake and coo or count their fingers for a while, but with Tally it's from deep sleep to screaming hunger in two seconds flat. We thought Mirri was going to be the biggest challenge but he's even better at disruption."

"Are you planning to have any more?" Pip asked.

"We weren't *planning* to have Tally—until suddenly we thought, why not—and we did."

Pip started to hum, looking into another life where she and a nice man might have thought *why not?*

"You can ask me whatever you want," Jillian said cheerfully.

"Really? You wouldn't find it intrusive?"

"Why would I? You're owed an explanation after my man abducted you."

"I did agree to visit his family," Pip said.

"Of course you did. Tane could get almost anyone to agree to almost anything."

"Except for Zach," Pip said. Immediately, she wished she hadn't. Zach had told her Tane propositioned him. He hadn't bound her over to secrecy, but telling Jillian was hardly cricket.

To her relief, Jillian laughed. "Zach's a treasure! He's so upright and *good*. Chivalrous, even. I always feel I could, and should, do better when I've spent time with Zach."

"He's human . . . right?"

"Oh yes, with the possible exception of an ancient ancestral dame he barely remembers. Her name was Shoshannah Rowan, and she told him stories that suggested a personal acquaintance with *over here*. She might have been fay . . . or just as likely fay-touched."

"Maybe she had a book called *Grandmother's Sunshine*," Pip said.

"Ask him!"

"Why, do you know it?" Pip wasn't sure whether she felt hopeful or wary. *Grandmother's Sunshine* had always seemed to be a private treasure for the Laurel family . . . and by extension for the de Leons and Pearmains.

"Not offhand, but Zach, being a teacher, has an interest in books for children." She added, reflectively, "It's very good for Tane not to get his own way all the time, but I'm not sure how much was willpower on Zach's part and how much was fear of upsetting that unnerving lover of his. My own dear Sam is possessive of her Oash, but Jisinia Peckerdale has her knocked into a cocked hat. Did Tane proposition you?"

"No—but Tam sort of did. Or implied it might have been on the cards, if I wanted."

"That's where he gets it from. You can always say no if the suggestion doesn't appeal."

"You didn't."

Jillian said calmly, "It *did* appeal. I met Tane at a vulnerable time of my life. He was exactly what I needed. He still is." In the faint light, Pip saw her swap the baby to the other side.

Pip said, "Which are you really? Jillian or Jules?"

"Both—though I spend more time in Jillian mode since the children already have a dad. I was Jules through my childhood, and up into my teens, and then I met Sherry—that's Sam's mum. Unfortunately, it didn't work out and I wasn't able to spend any time with Sam when she was little. Sam and I are on good terms now, and I'm gladder than I can say. Sherry is married, but I don't have contact with her because her man hasn't had disclosure. That's also the reason Sam doesn't see her mum these days."

"She'd keep quiet though, surely?"

"She probably would, but although Sherry's husband probably thinks she's very clever with the make-up, he might eventually *notice* that his stepdaughter doesn't look anywhere near the age she should."

"Did Sam's mum know about Jillian when you were together?"

"*I* didn't know about Jillian when I was with Shelley. Once I did—and a huge shock that was—it explained a few things. When I met Tane I told him about Jules fairly soon, but he didn't have a problem with it. He loves both my morphs although my *maid morph* as he puts it is more to his natural taste."

"But *how*? Why?"

"The best explanation I can get from Mum was that it was the sixties . . . though only just . . . and she met a lovely hippie girl called Paya, or something like it, at a party in a place in Sydney.

"I suspect that party was on the human side of the castle bridge gate, and possibly in the Treadwell terrace, though

Mum can't remember exactly.

"Paya wasn't feeling well, and Mum thought she'd had a bit too much to drink, so she took her out in the yard to get some air. They somehow got lost in a park and decided to bed down under the trees for the night. The lovely girl wasn't a girl, or not *only* a girl, and Mum got a bit more than she bargained for." Jillian laughed, and said thoughtfully, "At least, Mum *thinks* that's where I came from. As I said, it was the sixties and Mum was an original flower child, six or seven years before the term was invented. Bit of a free spirit, if you know what I mean—love is lovely, so take it when you find it."

"You can't be that old," Pip said.

"I'm sixty-two," Jillian said. "Sam's forty. Oash is around my age, I think. None of us looks our age because of the sylvan gene. I have no idea how old Mum is—she's nearly as slippery as Tane when it comes to dates and information. I always thought she was human normal, but as she's ageing . . . but not much . . . I've started suspecting my maternal grandad was probably at least part sylvan too. That would explain a few things, including Mum's penchant for sitting in waterfalls. We always thought *that* was just Zena being Zen.

"By the way, sylvan are a kind of offshoot of waterfolk. They age slowly and spend a lot of time in water. Oash is twenty or so years older than Sam, but because Sam has some human blood and Oash hasn't, they look about the same age." She detached her baby, who had evidently gone to sleep again. "I hope that's cleared up a few of your questions."

"It sort of has, but what about your children? Do any of them have other halves?"

"I don't know. I doubt it with Jane and Sulane, but it's not an exact science. They don't *look* underdeveloped or starved, and that's the way I was in my teens, despite Mum's assiduous mothering and a lot of grumpy doctors implying I was neglected. I absolutely wasn't! Sylvans and part-sylvans just don't *do* well in human society. Sam — hmm — she's bi, and she also had the starved look until she bloomed with her Oash, but she doesn't have an actual other self. Trae looks like his pisky grandad, so he might throw to the mutie line in a year or so. He hopes so, because Cousin Jamie is his hero, but who knows?

"It doesn't matter which way our children morph, or don't. We will expect it when we see it, and not if we don't, and we'll love them anyway."

"Sounds like our family," Pip said. She told Jillian about Little Mum, Little Dad and the others. She thought of it as quid pro quo, but in her deeper mind she knew she wanted them not to be forgotten. It was the only way to do her duty to the family.

Jillian chuckled. "You know what? I'm pretty sure I remember seeing you in a play when I was a kid. You were perched up in a tree in a park, staring down at characters behaving badly with *such* a disapproving expression."

"Really? I was about seven though, so you'd be three or so — oh, wait — do you mean the revival?"

"The what?"

"That play ran for a long time, and I remember we did a kind of extra performance outdoors during a festival. It might have been nineteen sixty-five. There were people sleeping in the park, and lots of guitars and flutes, and people making jewellery. I remember one jeweller, because his name was Lawrence Goldsmith. I thought that was funny. He was nice. I meant to show him my ring, but when I went back to his tent he wasn't there." She thought back, remembering. "You know, I can't even remember the name of that play. Isn't that silly?"

"I expect you just heard it being referred to as *the play*," Jillian said.

"That makes sense."

"Anyway, it was called *Lord What Fools.* I remember Mum telling me it was a quote from Shakespeare."

Aha.

Pip said, "So *that's* why I've been thinking it had something to do with Shakespeare. I didn't think it could be *A Midsummer Night's Dream* or *The Tempest*, but Shakespeare kept coming to mind."

Jillian got out of the chair, stretched, then said in a deeper voice, "Can I get you anything before I put Tally to bed, Miss Pearmain?"

Pip said, "No thank you," and snuggled down again.

Her mind was busy processing new information.

"By the way, you're welcome to stay with us for as long as you want. It's a mad house, but a happy one, and it's very good for our Jane to have another dancer to practise with," Jules said.

"I'd love to stay . . . but I have to be home to take a phone call from my agent on Monday morning."

CHAPTER NINE. ARDAL, TEAM TAM AND PATCHWORK NORA

Pip soon got into a routine of dance practice with Jane. She also went foraging with Sulane, who went out every day in search of mushrooms, nuts, and tubers. Sulane was a practical girl, less impulsive than Jane, and she had a sly sense of humour. Pip liked her a lot. She swam in the fossmere with opinionated little Mirri and met Liffey and Finn again, along with Finn's look-alike younger brothers, Rye and Lee.

She also met Ardal Cornfellow, the young man Jane referred to as *mine*. He was a stocky youth with fair curly hair who hugged Jane in greeting but who didn't kiss her. He informed Pip that he worked with horses and at the pottery, and he took her riding up in the chalklands, matching her with a silver-grey pony with a high opinion of itself. The lad said the pony's name was Fimber, and that he'd look after her because his consequence wouldn't allow him to drop a rider in the gorse.

Pip took his word for it.

Sulane, who wore less ethereal clothing than Jane, thoughtfully lent her what she called *knee-knickers* and a rust-coloured shirt matched with a divided skirt and soft boots for the exercise.

"Keep 'em," she said when Pip demurred. "They don't fit me anymore, and Mirri's even smaller than you. Besides, she *threw water,* so she probably won't ever bother much with clothes."

The chalklands were high and airy and as lovely as everywhere else Pip had seen during her Experience. She also saw manors set in stately grounds and a place Ardal said was called the castle.

"You have a king and queen?" she asked, staring at high and distant turrets. She thought this castle, or one very like it, had been illustrated in *Grandmother's Sunshine*. If she wasn't mistaken, the picture belonged to a story called *The Education of Tedwin*, which was about a fair-haired boy who kept stopping his work in the castle library to read the scrolls. He'd found a beautiful painting and walked a long way, looking for the waterfall it represented. He found it with the help of a golden child.

Goodness, that must have been a waterfolk child! Pip almost laughed in delight at her late-come understanding. That had been one of the longer stories in the book. Many of them occupied a single spread, but *The Education of Tedwin* had actual chapters.

Ardal had evidently noticed her abstraction, because he waited patiently until she looked up at him again before answering, "No, Mistress Pip. Courtfolk live there, and at t' manors."

"What are they? Are you one?"

Tedwin was one!

Ardal grinned at her, with his fair skin turning pink with either embarrassment or humour. "Nay, mistress, I'm a simple hob man. The courtfolk are elegant, like." He tugged at the peculiar garment he wore as if in explanation. It was like a grandpa shirt, but longer, and it was shirred and pleated down the front. It looked something like the shepherds' smocks some of the chorus had worn in the musical *Queen of the May*. Pip had played Fairweather Joan, the comic relief who had always looked on the bright side. She recalled one of the shepherds, 'Normous Geordie, had seized her and pulled her into a vigorous *pas de deux* in the final performance. He'd been almost two metres tall, so he'd had to hold her at chest height . . . The audience had loved it. So had Pip. The director . . . not so much. Neither had the actor who played Bess, the May Queen of the title. What had her name been . . . Selina Moon. Such a pretty girl. Pity her tolerance of being upstaged wasn't as long as her blonde hair.

She jerked out of her reflections. Ardal's smock was much nicer than the one 'Normous Geordie had worn, being ice blue and embroidered with ears of wheat.

The smock and the gesture didn't tell her much about his pedigree, but she thought it might not be polite to keep questioning people who had been so kind and friendly. Besides, she recalled she'd heard the term before. Jane had identified the pretty dancing tune as *Silk and Circumstance,* and she'd said *that* was courtfolk music. It sort of jelled with what she recalled of the story about Tedwin.

As for *simple,* she thought young Ardal was probably anything but. He was evidently interested in Jane, but she wasn't sure in what capacity. It seemed a little odd that he'd choose Jane, as Sulane seemed to share more of his concerns. Of course, she was just fourteen and she seemed to function as an older child rather than a teenager . . .

Ardal signalled that they might continue, and Fimber followed Indi, Ardal's bay mare, without any input from Pip. They rode gently across the chalklands, where clumps of fruit trees flourished, hung with small red apples. There were pear and plum trees too, but Ardal said their fruiting season was over. They stopped to pick apples, which they shared with Indi and Fimber.

Pip saw wildflowers, pink, white, and purple. She didn't know what they were, but she wished fervently that she could have photographed them to show to Little Mum.

Her phone was back in her messenger bag in *Tulpenmanie.*

Little Mum was gone, but Pip thought she'd still like a souvenir picture—no—a *lot* of souvenir pictures for herself. Why not ask Ardal? He, like everyone else she'd met in this lovely place, was friendly and generous with his time.

"Ardal, could I borrow your phone?"

She expected him to hand it over without delay.

Instead, he hesitated.

"Just to take a few photos," she said.

"Photos."

"Photographs."

"Ah!" His face lit with comprehension. "I've seen photographs. My Jane has some. But I don't have a phone . . . is that what you take photographs with? I thought that was a camera."

Pip might have thought he was mocking her, but he looked honestly perplexed. She remembered there was no electricity at the fossmere. Was that generally true of this place? "Ardal, where do you live?"

"At home with Mam and Dad and t'others . . . and Aunt Ebba and Uncle Pat and their lot live just across the way . . . nearer the pottery."

"Do you have electricity there?"

He drew his brows down. "Like . . . lightning?"

"No, do you have switches to boil kettles?"

"Nay, we use an iron griddle on t'range for that."

No electricity then, and since he doesn't know what it is, it must be general.

She'd noted there were no cars, and she'd seen nothing more advanced than the lanterns in the way of lighting.

Everyone here must live off the grid, without even generators.

So simple. And yet, Jane went to see her cousins, and Jillian Jules had lived for at least twenty years in the human realm. Tane self-evidently passed back and forth. Mama Tam had suggested she and her other sons and daughters never did.

Therefore . . .

"Ardal, do you ever go to the human realm? Where I live?"

He squished his mouth sideways as if in thought. "I *have* done. I've been to t'pub they call The Harvest Hob a time or three. Run by Master Applebee and his colleen. I have some hob cider, and it's good, but when I look outside . . ." He shrugged. "I couldn't see how to *be* there. So I come home w'out stepping forth. Mam says it's for the best. If I don't *feel* the place . . . better not to go." He gave her a sudden grin. "Besides, some maids from out there came in and *stared* at me. 'Twas reet scary."

"I expect they thought you were handsome," Pip said, trying for diplomacy.

"Get away with thee," Ardal said, still grinning.

"You're nice looking," Pip said truthfully. She had a feeling her attempt at politeness was going badly awry.

"I am that. Mam says I'm handsome enough to break a looking glass at fifty paces."

Pip had no idea what that meant, or how to respond, so she gave up.

Ardal said, "I'd lend you a phonie if I had one."

Pip thanked him and resolved to ask someone at the fossmere, possibly Jillian Jules, for clarification.

She expected to be stiff and sore after riding for the first time in decades, but ballet practice apparently kept her muscles fit for other activities. Or maybe it was swimming in the fossmere.

Once she had farewelled Ardal and the ponies, and left him conversing with Jane, Pip went to find Jillian Jules.

She found Jules standing with Tane and watching Mirri play with pebbles. Tane had the baby in his arms.

"Jules?"

He turned. "Hello, Miss Pearmain. How did you get along with that pony?"

"Fine. Ardal is going to take me out again tomorrow. Jane will come too, he hopes. He has a pony called Yearby he wants her to try."

"He's a good lad, and Jane knows it," Jules agreed.

Pip said, "I saw some wonderful scenery today. We went to the castle."

"That far! You must have impressed Ardal with your fortitude. "

"He checked that I was okay. I asked to borrow his phone."

Jules bit his lip.

"He hadn't a clue what I meant."

"No . . . he wouldn't have."

"You know, though."

"*I* do. I even have one. So does Tane, don't you, my love?"

Tane nodded, without looking away from his youngest daughter. "Doesn't work well though."

"That's because you *will* keep getting it in the water," his spouse said. It sounded like a well-worn dialogue.

"May I borrow one for tomorrow?"

"You would be welcome to, but it would be no use. They don't work here. There's no network, and besides . . . they just *don't*. I expect you've noted we don't use cars? If someone managed to get one through a gateway — and I don't know if anyone ever has — it would be no more than a hunk of metal and plastic. The metal might be okay, but the plastic would start cringing pretty soon. Batteries don't work here, and neither does anything electric . . . not even if it's solar powered."

"Whyever not?"

Jules said, "You may be sure I asked the same thing when this one lured me *over here* for the first time." He poked Tane in the ribs. "He claimed he didn't know."

"I don't," Tane protested.

"So, I asked Jory — that's Tane's half-brother through their dad, Merry.

"Jory lives human and always has. Unlike me, he didn't even know he had fay blood until he was man-grown. Anyway, he didn't know what was up with the batteries either. Finally, I got around to asking Merryn, which is what I should have done in the first place. Merry lives *over here*, but he *does* go human-side sometimes to hit up the markets or to visit his cousin and her man, or Jory's family . . . his wife, Rachel, is friends with Linda's mum . . . anyway, Merry is what you might call mercurial, but he has more sense in his head than *some* people I might name." He jerked his thumb at Tane who blew a raspberry in return.

Jules went on, "Merry said Rach thinks it's to do with the industrial revolution. Yes, I know it sounds mad. It seems that before that, there was a lot of coming and going between here and there, because there wasn't much difference in the lifestyles. Once the human-side went over to machinery, it forced the communities apart, because anyone who brought machines over here soon discovered they wouldn't — couldn't — work. Conversely, anyone from here already knew *going* won't work in the human realm.

"So, my phone is just metal and plastic here. It won't turn on. It can hold its integrity as long as I take it through the gates every month or so to remind it of what it is and what it's supposed to do. Once I step through the castle bridge gate, or the pixie forest one for that matter, it buzzes to life and starts madly doing its updates. It reminds me of a woman who's spent a month in the outback and suddenly realises she needs to comb her hair and put on something that isn't coloured with red dust.

"If I step back through the gate — flat as a tack in an instant. It's so flat that it uses no battery power at all. If it has nineteen percent battery when I step through to here, I can stay a month and step back . . . and it will still have that nineteen percent. We don't really know why, so Merry's and Rachel's explanation seems as good as ever."

"Oh. What about cameras?"

"The really old mechanical cameras work, but most people won't stand still long enough to be photographed. Painting and sketching are the usual portrait media *over here*. Tane and I have photos of the kids, though. My mum made sure of that. She hustles us all through a gate in our Sunday best a couple of times a year to get recorded. Her place is full of collages all tastefully decorated with seashells and dried herbs and such. She gives us an album every Christmas."

"Oh," Pip said again.

"We might be able to find someone with one of those old cameras if you like. There's a pixie man over at KerryKenny who has one. Friend of Sam's. He'd lend it."

"No, never mind. Thanks anyway."

Pip blew out her cheeks. No electricity *at all*.

Frankly, she hadn't missed it.

The next day, after Pip rode out with Ardal and Jane, Finn and Liffey offered a trip to a local leprechaun village with the beguiling name of Smile o' the Glean.

Pip, avid for any new and interesting sight, agreed happily. They took her hands, one on each side, and stepped out into the familiar fuzz of *going*.

Pip was getting used to being led about like a child. Holding hands *over here* was so common she hardly even thought about it anymore. Various people had explained to her that it was necessary to ensure everyone in a group arrived at the same place at the same time . . . unless, of course, everyone in the group knew the way.

The village was picture-book pretty, with a mix of white-washed cottages and others built of the local grey stone. Each dwelling had its garden of flowers, fruit and vegetables. Cows, much smaller than those Pip had seen at home, roamed at will.

There was even an inn, a low-profiled building that looked very old. Pip didn't go inside, because most people appeared to prefer being out, seated on stools or long forms around rustic tables.

It was there that she met Team Tam. She was never sure if it was by arrangement or simply by casual chance. The men greeted them with cheerful nods, but that seemed pretty much the way everyone acknowledged everyone else around here.

Tane's father Merryn was much as she expected, smiling and mercurial in a pisky kilt like his son's.

William Croft was a large, slow-spoken and gentle man clad in the biggest grandpa shirt she'd ever seen . . . even more voluminous than Ardal's.

Moss the Beechmaster was dark and quiet with a strong air of calm authority. He didn't wear any clothing apart from some kind of band confining his long hair, which startled Pip a little, although she was getting used to the absence of garments at the fossmere. Liffey told her softly that Moss was a tree lad, and that this was the proper term for a treefolk man of any age. He was the master of the beech clan—a term that meant little to Pip, but which sounded imposing. His stillness and dignity went a long way to explaining why Mama Tam had chosen him to give her a daughter.

The fourth man of Team Tam was introduced as Liam Dancey. He was the one who had married Tam and fathered her three younger children, the halfling leprechaun sons. It was lucky for Pip that she'd encountered Finn often enough to see beyond the green tone of his skin to the charming young man he was, because Liam was much greener than any of his sons. He was small, like Mama Tam, so Pip decided there must be a taller ancestor somewhere to give Finn his extra height. Like William Cliff, Liam was clad from collar to toes, wearing soft brown garments sewn with four silver wavy lines on the sleeve.

Pip asked him about that.

He beamed at her, tapping the first and longest of the lines. "This one is to tell of me lovie, darlin' Tam. Since she said she'd have me I've worn her water sign with pride on ivery shirt to me name." He touched the other three, which were half the length of the first. "These tell of me fine gossoons, and me love and pridefulness. Half-water they are, see? Look closer and ye'll note green in the other half to show they're men o' the green way as well."

Pip looked closer.

Liam nodded approval and tapped a spot beneath the lines where Pip now perceived a single silver stitch and three green ones. "This now — this is for the sweet colleen me son Finn planted in darlin' Liffey." He beamed and nodded, before confiding, in a lower voice, "Tis me ambition to live long and well enough to sport a whole sleeve full o' stitches and call meself *athair na milliúin*." He gave her another sly grin, bent forward, and whispered, "Father o' millions to ye . . ."

Pip smiled and wished him well with his ambition. She wasn't sure if Finn had heard but she did note folk of *the green way*, as Liam styled himself, had an unusually forthright way of expressing themselves.

On the whole, she approved.

After she'd drunk healths with Team Tam in a tiny glass of hob cider with a tinier drop of leprechaun poteen, Liffey and Finn conducted her through the village, introducing her here and there as *Mistress Pip, from* over there, *who is staying at the fossmere*. She lost count of the people, green-skinned men and rosy women, who wished her *a fine life and may the luck of the green way attend ye*. She finally settled for a smile and a nod, since she had trouble getting her tongue around some of their names. The first names were not so bad, being mostly what she thought of as *stage Irish*, but some of the surnames were exceedingly odd.

She discovered later that this was because teenaged lepre-
chauns chose their own, which might be anything from a simple descriptor such as *Hill, Singer,* or *Milkmaid* to a long and
poetic phrase.

The high point of the visit, apart from Tam's Team, was
seeing a cat who looked just like Amberjill, sprawled on a
warm stone doorstep. It gave her a turn, but one of the
women, whom she now understood to be termed *colleens*, informed her, *the baste's name is Patchwork Nora.*

Pip gazed into autumn eyes, and Patchwork Nora gazed
back.

"Good day to you, Patchwork Nora," Pip said civilly.

The cat twitched her tail, then her whiskers. *Road rise, friend
of my blood.*

Pip felt her eyebrows shoot skywards.

"You know Cat-Morse!"

Patchwork Nora tilted an ear twenty degrees to the east.

Child of the seanbhanríon, we invented it.

Pip would have lingered to talk, but Liffey and Finn had
gone on ahead. The woman who had introduced her to the
calico said softly, "Ah, the one has spoken wid ye. Best ye go
on now."

"Okay," Pip said, blinking.

The woman looked her over with bi-coloured eyes that
suddenly reminded Pip of someone.

"Are you related to a young woman named Jisinia?" she
asked.

"I am that . . . kin cousin to Calypso Lindon . . . her mam,
that is." She smiled. "You've met with that one, then?"

Pip agreed that she had.

The woman said, "Should ye have the ear of her again, tell
her Branna Pusheen wants to see her *before* she takes up the
paddy chalice."

"I will." Pip added, "Pusheen? I don't think I've heard that name before."

"Why should ye indeed? *Little cat,* they called me when I was knee high, and so I took it for my own."

Pip puzzled over this pronouncement as she hurried after Liffey and Finn. Fortunately, they were walking in the normal fashion.

There was so much to do in the fay homeland, and so much to learn! So many things she'd made a note to ask her hosts, but without her feint-lined pad and her old exercise books, she would never remember them.

Chapter Ten. Timetable

Pip had finished her morning dancing practice with Jane and Trae, when she turned to find Tane watching them with affectionate amusement.

"Ready, lovie?"

"What for?" Pip blurted, as she belatedly realised he was talking to her.

Tane said, "I promised to take you to Hob's Island."

So he had.

Pip said, suspiciously, "There is a boat involved, right?"

He nodded. "I borrowed it from Robin Cottman—he's a semi brother to Linda."

Pip tried, and failed, to remember who Linda was. Instead, she said, "Does Master Cottman know you borrowed it?" She discovered that was the correct honorific for most males *over here.*

"Probably not, but he won't mind—are you coming?"

Pip started to hum. She'd intended to ask Ardal to take her riding again that morning if she could find him. She had her heart set on learning to jump.

Jules came up, dressed in cotton shorts and a T-shirt saying *I'm in two minds . . .* on the front. "I can come too, if you don't trust yourself around this one." He jerked his thumb at Tane. Before Pip could take offence, he added, "I gather Tane promised you this trip when he abducted you, and it really has to be this morning."

"Why?" Pip expected them to say something learned about tides, but Jules said, "You had to be back in Jellico Bay by

67

eight o'clock on Monday morning, I think?"

Pip swayed back on her bare heels. She'd forgotten that.

She wanted to say it didn't matter, but she remembered she'd made it clear to Trip that she had to be back for a very important call.

"What's today?" she asked with a sinking feeling in her stomach.

"Sunday, and around eight o'clock," Jules said, shoving his hands in his pockets.

Pip thought again how unlike Jillian he was in his mannerisms. As Jillian, he was motherly, but Jules behaved more like a loving uncle. As Jillian had said, the children already had a dad.

Pip had noticed the older children addressed him and referred to him by his first name.

None of my business if they have three parents to love them. I had six grandparents. And now I have twenty-four hours . . .

Pip dismissed that comforting thought immediately. Before she could take that call from Magda Saxer, she had to fit in the visit to the island, farewell her temporary family, get back through the underwater gateway and rendezvous with *Tulpenmanie,* sail a few hours back to the beach where she'd embarked, meet Jamie and get driven back to Lemonwood Cottage.

When she thought of all the things she had to do before the call, she wondered if she'd left it too late already. She wondered if she really cared.

There *might* be a shortcut.

"Liffey told me there are quite a few gateways, including one not far from the castle. Would it be possible to go home through one of those instead of reversing the rigmarole it took to get me here?"

Jules said, "It would be, but then you'd have to catch a plane or a ferry to get home."

"Oh. Why?"

"There's a gateway in Sydney—that's the one Liffey meant—one at Dancing Tor and another one at Fiddle Bay, as well as a handful in Victoria, including the oak door, the St Botolph's gate, and the pixie forest one my Sam uses," Jules said, ticking them off. "There's one in the chalklands where the Cornfellows live that takes you through to a pub in Adelaide. Oddly enough there don't seem to be any accessible ones in Tasmania, unless you count the one in Bass Strait, and as you undoubtedly discovered, that's a fair sail from land. It's also a bit of a mongrel to access. You need someone with enough water blood to get you through, and that person has to be able to *pass*. That combination is fairly rare. Come to think of it, Tane is the only one I know for sure who can do it without feeling or giving discomfort."

Pip sighed, as her available time concertinaed again. "How can we fit all this in?" she asked plaintively.

Jane said, "Trae and I worked out a timetable Miss Pearmain. We'll have a dip in the fossmere. I'll bring breakfast while you get dry. Then Dadda and Jules can take you to the island in Master Cottman's boat. After that, Dadda will take you down safely through the gateway, and Jules will bring Master Cottman's boat back. Then *you* can go with Jin and Zach, who will hand you on to Jamie, who will drive you home."

"Leaving Tane to come back here, as long as he doesn't stop off to flirt with fishermaids," Jules said.

Tane kissed Jane on the brow. "You've worked it all out beautifully, Janie."

Jane gave him a hug. A squall from behind made them all turn to see Sulane approaching with the baby. "Jules—"

"Yes, I'd better feed the bottomless pit while Miss Pearmain goes to the fossmere," Jules said, holding out his arms for his baby. He kissed the child, and when he raised his head, it was Jillian. She smiled at Pip. "Don't worry, Pip. If Trae and

Jane worked it out, there *will* be time. One of their grandads is a pisky man—though the lord alone knows exactly what the other one is—and what piskies don't know about numbers isn't worth knowing."

Chapter Eleven. Dolphins

Master Cottman's boat proved to be a sturdy dinghy. Pip, feeling a little bereft already after leaving the children and the beautiful fossmere, and her dancing ground, and—well, everything—looked down from where she stood on the cliff path.

Tane leaped lightly into the boat then made a theatrical gesture and held out his arms for Jules. "Jump, beloved! I'll catch you!"

Jules rolled his eyes at Pip. "My husband has a peculiar sense of humour."

"Husband?"

Tane laughed. "I wed both of them before the old red cat. Couldn't have my Jewel feeling left out."

"I'm sure he doesn't," Pip said.

"Drop the act, love," Jules said. He held up his hand, showing Pip a braided ring on his wedding finger. It wasn't the same as the one Jillian wore, but it had two twists as hers did, while Tane's had three.

Beautiful rings. Pip felt a pang for her heaven and earth ring, but she knew she'd feel a greater one if she'd not acted on her desire to leave something of herself behind.

Tane grinned, looking like a naughty schoolboy, and held out his arms to Pip instead.

She glanced at Jules.

"Go for it. You might even enjoy it."

"You mean jump?" Pip clarified.

"If you feel up to it. He won't drop you."

"It's not the first time," Pip observed. If they thought she meant being in Tane's keeping, that was their business. She counted down as Jane had and sprang into his waiting arms.

He gave her a friendly hug, set her down, and reached up to help Jules.

"I've *told* you," Jules said, hopping into the boat. "Who's rowing?"

"I'll do it." Tane settled in the seat and unshipped the oars.

The trip over the water to the island was short and delightful. Pip felt her head was on a swivel as she gazed into clear, green depths, watched gulls bobbing on waves and saw the chalk cliffs recede, looking like a petrified curtain. She'd never been to Dover or to the Cliffs of Moher, but she'd seen pictures of them, and she thought the chalk cliffs even more imposingly beautiful.

She kept a secret watch for the seaman, Lore Mor Arlodh and his intrepid wife. Instead, she saw real dolphins leaping and twisting in an aerial ballet.

Had anyone written a ballet about dolphins?

I could try out some choreography in my practice tomorrow.

The thought brought a surge of excitement.

I'd need music. Darn it! Why didn't I think of this before? I could have asked Trae!

The idea of asking a twelve-year-old boy in a kilt to suggest suitable ballet music should have seemed incongruous.

I'll ask Magda Saxer if she has anyone on her books who does music. It needs to be bright and dramatic, then ethereal . . . maybe "Silk and Circumstance" could be adapted to the first act. I'll get that recording of Tamzin Campania's Magic Fiddle.

Her mind scurried on, suggesting this and that. *Maybe I could go to the Jellico Bay school and ask if any of the children would like to learn some simplified ballet. We could do a performance for the parents. It would be the way it was when I went to Apples and Pears with Angie Blake.*

She knew untrained children would need *very* simple

steps, but the music would help. Costumes could be grey leotards. Would the school be interested? She'd never made any effort to integrate into the Jellico Bay community.

I have to ask.

Tane's jewellery clinked faintly as he rowed, and he seemed to be putting in less effort than the speed suggested.

Pip wanted to tell the men her notion, and to ask their advice, but she had no idea how they'd react. Jules had been brought up on the human side of the gates, but how long was it since he'd spent much time there? Why would he, when he had all this—his children, Tane and a place of outstanding beauty and harmony to live?

That T-shirt came from a shop. *Or maybe from one of those places where you can custom-design your own clothes. Tane goes around markets with his father and his – what – cousin-by-love?*

As they neared the island, Jules asked, "What's the deal with wanting to come here, Miss Pearmain?"

Chapter Twelve. Iris's Wishing Well

Pip oriented on what Jules had said, and admitted, "I'm not sure what you mean."

"There must be a reason you wanted to come here, particularly. You surely haven't been here before."

"There is a good reason, but it's mixed up in my mind. I have a bucket list."

"I see." Jules sounded deadpan. He was rather good at that.

"You don't." Pip stretched out her legs and admired her feet. Something . . . maybe dancing on the faintly abrasive chalk, or maybe the bracing water of the fossmere, had left her toenails looking pristine for the first time in years.

The bucket list had been a long-held secret, shared only with her cousins, the cats and Zach, but she felt comfortable telling it to Jules and Tane. She thought they were probably used to secrets.

"I see." This time, Jules sounded as if he did see.

"I told Zach about it on *Tulpenmanie,* and he said he knew about a bucket on an island at a place called Iris's Wishing Well. He mentioned a lemon tree. Then I got distracted by something or other." She frowned, trying to recall. "And you mentioned an island, Tane, so I suppose I conflated the two in my head."

The men exchanged amused glances.

Nettled, Pip said, "I think I have a right to conflation and confusion. Changing your shape or playing about underwater and kidnapping old ladies might be normal for you two, but *I'm* human."

"Not laughing at you, lovie," Tane said.

"Just wondering why you think you're conflated and confused," Jules added. "And by the way, what old lady has my man kidnapped now? What's he done with her?"

Pip sighed. Jules was just four years shy of her age, but he looked a good quarter century younger.

She ignored his quip, and continued, "I'm confused because Zach was talking about an island in Bass Strait. I'd never heard of it, but there are *dozens* of islands in the Furneaux Group alone. Then there's Hypatia, and — I suppose, Iris's Wishing Well must be another of them. I've never seen it on a map, so it must be tiny."

Jules said, "I think you're confused about being confused, Miss Pearmain. Zach was undoubtedly talking about Hob's Island. There's a cottage there with a well belonging to Iris Cottman, Robin Cottman's mother. There is a lemon tree nearby."

"That would be the one we pee on ceremonially," Tane added cheerfully.

"But Zach's human."

Jules shrugged. "Humans visit *over here*, sometimes intentionally and sometimes — not. Zach's first visit was of the *not* variety."

"Oh?"

He shook his head. "Not my story to tell, and Tane, if you open that handsome mouth of yours to divulge Zach's business, then you *will* regret it."

Pip sighed over their double act. "So, I'm going to see a bucket."

She started to hum in her high-pitched happy buzz.

Her V-S Experience had been wonderful so far, and now she would see a bucket to add to her collection.

And I'll decoupage one when I get home, she promised herself, although she did feel learning decoupage might feel a shade *infra dig* after learning to ride in the chalklands and diving through the fossmere.

Tane shipped the oars, and the dinghy slid gently onto a sandy shore.

Jules got out and pulled the boat higher up before offering his hand to Pip.

She accepted it and stepped a bit unsteadily out. "Coming?" Jules asked Tane.

Tane grinned and shook his head. "I'll wait here, lovies. You can do the honours for that tree." He settled back and was instantly asleep.

Jules shook his head and walked up the beach. "Come on Miss Pearmain."

Pip followed, digging her bare toes into the fine white sliding grains. She had on the divided skirt Sulane had donated, which was perfect for free movement. She'd left the boots behind in the dinghy.

"Why do you call me *Miss Pearmain*?" she asked, hurrying to catch up with her guide.

Jules countered, "What should I call you?"

"Jillian calls me Pip sometimes."

"Ah, but you call her Jillian."

"Does that mean I ought to call you Mister . . . Master . . . what's your last name, anyway?"

Jules stopped walking. "That's a bit of a conundrum. Mum's original name was Fraeman. She obviously never married my father, whether he was the delightful Paya or someone else, but she has since married Sedge Essden, who is a pixie man who *lives human*. They met after I'd left home, so Sedge never felt the need to adopt me. He did, however, inform me I could call him *Dad* if I ever felt the emotional need of a father."

"Do you?"

"No. I call him Sedge. He's a nice bloke — Mum's happy

with him. I wish she'd met him when I was younger, but then, he's only a bit older than I am, so it wouldn't have worked."

"Name?" Pip reminded.

"I went by Jules Fraeman then later by Jillian Fraeman, but I'm now frequently styled Jillian Jules. Jillian also calls herself Mistress Jillian Pendennis when she's feeling stately, but that doesn't work so well for *me*." He indicated himself. "Neither can I call myself Tane's wife, because that would imply I'm gay — a gaylord, as they put it *over here*."

"Aren't you?" Pip asked, fascinated.

Jules said, testily, "No, I'm not. I can see why you would think so, but I'm *not*. I'm not even bi, the way my Sam is. I love Tane and I do sleep with him, if you'll pardon the euphemism, but I've never been drawn to any other man in my life. If I strayed, which is considered a quaint concept around these parts, it would be with a woman. So far, I haven't wanted to. Not that any of that matters *here*.

"The family — including Tane's brothers and sisters, and all the extended Pendennis mob — accept us, just as they accept Sam and Oash's arrangement. The children don't mind in the least. Obviously, sometimes only a mother will do . . . as when Tallien is howling for sustenance . . . but Jillian is always available in a blink. And if I could do it over, I'd still choose the same path. Even the debacle with Sam's mum, Sherry — and *what* a debacle that was — brought us Sam and Oash, and my first granddaughter, whom we all love dearly. I've been far more fortunate than I could have hoped for, and probably more so than I've deserved."

"I'd better call you Jules then," Pip said, taking a few steps backwards to ward off more explanations and emotions. She didn't *think* Jules was about to weep with thankfulness, but she certainly wasn't about to encourage him. She added, "Not that it matters what I call you. After today we'll probably never meet again."

Jules gave her his sudden wicked grin. "Mistress Pippin, whyever would you think that?"

"Because getting here is so complicated, and my Experience was a one-shot deal."

"That's right, you're here on a V-S voucher."

"How did you—oh, of course. Tane is Jamie's uncle, and that makes you—"

"His aunt-by-love, sometimes, and his friend otherwise. He's a good lad, kind and surprisingly sweet natured."

"My voucher time is nearly up," she reminded him.

"Yes, but do you *really* think we, your fossmere family, and especially Jane, will be happy never to see you again? Jane admires you enormously and you've been wonderful for her."

Pip felt her face go slack with amazement.

"Laura, Jamie's sister, has taught her some ballet, and now she's seen someone with life-long ballet experience who is still devoted to the craft. You may depend that Jane will find a way to dance with you again. And if she decides to pay you a visit at your home, there's not much we can do to stop her. She'll be of age very soon, and she *will* pry your address out of Jamie. He's only a few months older than she is, and Jane will flim-flam him into thinking she had it and has momentarily misplaced it in her brain. Mind you, if young Master Cornfellow gets what *he's* angling for, you might get a visit from him as well. I hope you have a spare room and a tolerant nature."

"He said he was a hob," Pip said uncertainly.

"He is a pureblood hob, and hobs are renowned for getting what they aim for. They don't push . . . they just gently encroach until you're in their arms and getting lost in those preposterous smocks they insist on wearing. *Not* speaking from experience, by the way, but I know a fair few of them. Young Master Cornfellow has been aiming for our Jane since they met at a ceilidh back when she was sixteen."

"I hope Jane is happy with that."

"Jane is also renowned for getting what she aims for," Jules said. He must have seen an odd expression pass over Pip's face because he grinned again. "Miss Pear . . . Mistress Pip, our Jane is the sweetest, most loving maid anyone could want as a daughter, but she's also as stubborn as the day is long. If Ardal Cornfellow says *will you*, and if she says *yes*, then it will because she's had her heart set on him for quite a while. If she hasn't, then he'll never get to say *will you*."

Pip nodded vaguely and began to walk on. She understood Jane's point of view perfectly. *She* was also as stubborn as the day was long. She wondered why so few people had ever noticed.

The island was large enough to carry grass and trees above the tideline, and Pip saw gulls and other birds fossicking around where the sand and pebbles met the soil. She was startled when they reached a hut surrounded by a cottage garden.

The hut was built of stone, with a slate roof. The garden, although smaller, reminded Pip of the one she tended at Lemonwood Cottage. There was the same riot of nasturtiums in multiple colours, the same befrilled pansies, and faded tomato vines, vast tracts of cornstalks and pumpkins in yellow, green and startling orange. The herb garden flourished with smoke blue lavender, darker rosemary, and a mass of different coloured thymes mingled with mint and parsley. She saw a bed of German camomile, an olive tree and — yes, there was a stout lemon tree, bearing flowers and fruit together.

"Are you really going to pee on that?" she asked Jules.

"I am. It provides nitrogen."

"Am I expected to do it too?"

"Well, *I* don't," Jillian said with a giggle.

Pip blinked, and when she opened her eyes, Jules was back. She swallowed and turned her back, scanning about for the—*aha!* There was the well. She hurried over to inspect it, hoping Jules would attend to the lemon while she was elsewhere. She considered herself broadminded, but seeing a man who wasn't always a man libating on a lemon tree was a bit more than she was prepared to stomach.

The well looked like a bigger and more practical version of the wishing well she'd bought from Donovan Clancy's estate. It was about waist high, set in a circular stone coping, and when she peeped into the water, she detected a faint, sweet scent. It smelled like lemon blossom.

"Wind up a drink if you like," Jules said from behind her.

Evidently, he'd finished his business with the tree.

To Pip's assessing gaze, the lemon tree looked contented. Its oval leaves shone like patent leather, and its white and yellow flowers with the dusty-pink buds might have been moulded from royal icing. The fruit was large and well-rounded, but it lacked the bulging threat of the sentient lemon at home. It also appeared to lack the thorns.

"I have a lemon tree, but it's not as friendly as this one—in fact, not friendly at all," she said. "Do you think Jamie would pee on it for me if I ask? I told him his dog could, if it dared, but I didn't think to say he could, too."

"I expect he's already had a go," Jules said. "Have you met the dog?"

"No. He didn't have it with him, which is odd, since he said—or implied—he'd have it at my place while he's sitting with the cats. He said it was civilised."

"Hmm." Jules sucked in his lips.

"What?"

"Just—hmm."

"Jules, do I have to—" She recalled what Liffey had threatened to do to Finn, or maybe what Finn had suggested. "Do I have to twist that long nose of yours?"

Jules folded his arms and stood up straight. "You can

always try. If you think you can reach."

Pip said, dryly, "You might be surprised how high this lady can leap. But I won't. Just tell me one thing."

"I might."

"Is this another of those *dum-dum-dum* moments?"

"I expect so."

Pip grumped at him. Then she took hold of the handle of the well and started winding up a pail of water on the windlass.

She held her breath, anticipating her first sight of the bucket, and she wasn't disappointed.

It was perfect.

Pip wanted to embrace it, and the garden, and the island, and the whole beauty of *over there*.

She couldn't manage that, and so she did the next best thing. She embraced Jules, who laughed and kissed the top of her head.

After that, she gazed at the bucket until the tears stopped blurring her eyes. She scooped out some water in her hands and drank it. Then she splashed her face.

"All right, Mistress Pip?" Jules asked as she turned, blotting her cheeks with the hem of her shirt.

"Yes. Obviously. Of course. Why wouldn't I be? But I think it's time to go home."

CHAPTER THIRTEEN. INTERLUDE

April 2022

The trip home felt surreal.

Jules rowed them back to a point midway between the island and the cliffs and paused, backwatering until Tane nodded.

Tane got to his feet and reached out casually to Pip. "Ready, lovie?"

"Mistress Pip is ready for anything." Jules sounded sincere as he handed Pip's riding boots to Tane. He attached them somehow to his kilt, possibly by threading the laces through some of the charms.

"I can't take those. The salt water will kill them," Pip objected.

"Not a bit of it," Jules said cheerfully. "Just swill them with fresh water when you can, stuff them with springy-weed . . . no, newspaper . . . and leave them to dry. Rub a wee bit of oil into the uppers and you'll be all set."

Bucket oil. Pip felt happy about making up a batch after all.

"Thanks," she said to Jules.

Tane gave Pip air, and hand-in-hand they jumped into the water.

Pip intended to have a last look about at her beautiful fairyland, but Tane took them down and straight through the gateway without delay. It was daylight this time.

Pip *felt* the change as they passed through into the human realm. The water was colder, and it stung with salt.

They broke surface and Pip spluttered, amazed to see *Tulpenmanie's* hull looming over them.

"They're here!"

"Why wouldn't they be?" Tane asked. He added, wickedly, "Want to squeal now?"

Pip drew in a deep, unassisted breath and squealed, channelling Banshee Mary.

She was pleased to discover she still had the lungpower for it. She ventured a higher pitch and let it reverberate through the sky.

The old girl's still got it . . . Oops.

She'd swallowed a mouthful of Bass Strait.

Movement above translated itself into Jin and Zach, leaning over to stare down at them.

Jin made an impatient motion.

Zach bundled an armful of rope ladder overboard.

Pip pondered the possibilities of getting onto the ladder from the water, but Tane grasped her around the hips and hoisted her up as he had at the chalk cliffs. She climbed to the top, where Jin took her by the hands and steadied her as she clambered aboard.

"Phew!"

"Indeed," Jin said, gazing at her with impassive jewelled eyes.

Zach leaned over the side and called, "Tane, are you coming aboard?"

"What do you think?" Tane blew them all a kiss. "Incoming!" Pip's riding boots landed neatly on the deck. "Adieu, Miss Pearmain. Good luck with the phone call. I'll see you again." He submerged.

"That's a *no* then," Jin observed. She added, "And I thought *I* was rackety."

She and Zach stared at Pip.

"Are you okay, Miss Pearmain?" Zach ventured.

"Perfectly. And I think you'd better call me *Pip*, don't you? I hope you got Tane's note?" Pip bent to pick up her boots.

"We did," Jin said sourly. "It could hardly have been less communicative, but we gathered he'd made you an offer and you hadn't refused."

"I didn't refuse, but I didn't exactly know the extent of what I was agreeing to."

"That's Tane for you."

Zach said, "Actually, I'm surprised he left a note at all. I expect that was your idea?"

"It was. He'd given me figs and fixed my ring, so I assumed he was user-friendly."

"Hmm." Zach glanced at her hands.

Jin said, "You probably want a shower and some dry clothes. Whatever is that you're wearing?"

"Sulane gave it to me." Pip executed a runway turn. "Like it?"

"It suits you. It looks as if it was tailored especially."

"It's handy. And I've had such a wonderful time. I've been riding and swimming, and foraging. I've sat in a waterfall and drunk something scary with four lovely men—five if you count Finn."

"Did you get your ballet practice?" Jin asked.

"Yes. *With* live music. And I have an idea for a new ballet. *And*, guess what?"

"What?" Jin handed her a towel which she'd acquired from somewhere.

Pip said blissfully, "I have a brand-new bucket to add to my list! By the way, do you have enough fresh water for me to rinse my boots?"

"I'll deal with them," Zach said, taking possession.

Pip stood dripping on the deck for a happy few seconds before the cool April breeze reminded her she was back *human-side,* as Jules had put it. She raised both hands to push back her soggy hair. "I think I need a shower."

"Good plan," Jin said. "Your things are in the chart room."

"Thanks." Pip was about to descend when she thought of something. "Jin, do you know a woman named Branna Pusheen?"

Jisinia nodded warily. "She's my mother's cousin. Why?"

"She told me to tell you she wants to see you *before* you take up the paddy chalice."

"Oh," Jin said.

Zach, still holding the boots, gave her a puzzled look.

"That's what she said," Pip added.

Jisinia's cheeks turned slowly red.

PART TWO. DEBRIEFING AT LEMON-WOOD COTTAGE

April 2022

CHAPTER ONE. GRILLING JAMIE

Pip arrived back at Lemonwood Cottage at five o'clock.
Zach delivered her to the shore, where Jamie waited, leaning on the V-S vehicle.

Pip said goodbye to Zach and waved to Jin, who had remained on *Tulpenmanie*. She'd clammed up after Pip delivered the message. Not that she was naturally loquacious anyway.

Pip turned to Jamie, who had politely opened the rear door.

"I'm coming in the front with you."

"I'm not allowed—"

Pip cut him off. "My destination was to be a surprise, but this is just a waystation. I *know* I'm going home now, so it can't matter if I see the scenery. Besides, I want to grill you."

Jamie shrugged. "All right. But if Gerry fires me . . ."

"Who's Gerry?"

"Gerry. Geraint Trip. He's Grandma's husband, my step grandad."

"Ah, so your grandma is called Mary? I remember him mentioning her."

He nodded.

"I expect your grandma loves you a lot?"

"Yes." He didn't add *of course*. He didn't need to.

"Then Trip won't fire you. Anyway, I'll sort him out if he tries. I'll hum at him."

Jamie smiled. "I can just see you doing it."

"Even if I have to stand on a chair to do it."

He shook his head. "Gerry's not very big. Neither is Grandma. And Aunt Amaryllis is just a handspan taller than you. A *small* handspan."

"What about your mum?"

"She's tall, like me. See?" He produced his phone, thumbed through his gallery and presented Pip with a picture of a brown-haired woman who managed to be both beautiful and difficult to describe.

"And this is Dad."

Jamie's dad didn't look like Tane, but Pip thought she would have known they were related. They shared a cheerfully rackety look. Jory Pendennis had shaggy hair and a short silver earring. The tips of his ears came to a pronounced point.

"Hmph." Pip turned to have another look at Jamie. His ears were no more than *interesting*. He hardly looked like a fairy at all, save for the clear skin and luminous eyes — okay, he did look like a fairy after all.

So he has a mix of tall and short ancestry . . . like Jan and Lupin, she thought.

Pip gave the phone back. It occurred to her that *hmph* might not be the best thing to have said, so she added, "I like the look of your parents."

"So do I. They shouldn't go together, but they do."

Pip quite saw what he meant. Jory Pendennis looked rackety. His wife Linda didn't. Probably that meant they balanced themselves out nicely.

She walked around the vehicle and got in the front.

Jamie closed the back door and joined her. "Was that the end of the grilling?" he asked hopefully.

"Not even close," Pip said.

She waited until Jamie navigated the narrow side road that had led to the shore and turned onto a B road before she began the grilling proper.

"Where's your dog? I hope you didn't leave him with the

cats without supervision?"

"No."

"Then where is he?"

"I've never been sure," Jamie responded.

He sounded evasive, but Pip had no sense he was lying.

She shifted to something else. "Have you been peeing on my lemon tree?"

She watched with interest as his fair-skinned face turned pink.

So fairies blushed. That made two of them.

"Good. Jules seemed to think it would be beneficial for it. By the way, has Jane been in touch with you?"

"Not lately."

"Jules suggested she might pry my address out of you at some point."

"I won't tell her."

"I don't mind if you do, but *if* you do, I want it to be because you've made an informed decision and not because she's wheedled it out of you."

"Jane wouldn't do that."

"I wouldn't have thought so, but Jules says she would."

Jamie glanced at her. "How did you get along with Uncle Tane?"

"We got on well, considering he vanished, so I almost called triple zero, then he trod on my leg, lured me up on deck and plied me with figs."

"That doesn't sound *too* terrible," Jamie said cautiously.

"That was *before* he scooped me up in his arms and jumped overboard and abducted me to fairyland."

She waited for Jamie's reaction, which was disappointingly bland.

"You don't seem surprised."

"I'm not, really. You implied you'd met Jane, which suggests a trip through the underwater gateway."

"Darn, you would pick up on that."

"So, how did you enjoy your Experience, aside from being Taned and Janed?" Jamie ventured.

"I loved it *all*. Aside from the triple zero bit. It was magical, wonderful, glorious, and I almost got propositioned by a beautiful older lady in a pool."

"That'd be Mama Tam."

"It was. Exactly what relation is she to you?"

Jamie was quiet for a few seconds, probably working it out. "By love, or by blood?"

"Either."

"Well, Tane and my dad, Jory, are half-brothers. Grandad Pendennis is their father. Dad's mother is Grandma Rachel, and Mama Tam is Uncle Tane's mother, so she's a kind of granny-by-love but nothing by blood."

"So, you don't loiter in waterfalls or — Jamie, exactly what *are* you?"

He countered, "What are you?"

"Human."

"Well, I'm half-human. Grandma Mary and Grandma Rachel are human. Grandad Pendennis is a pisky man and my grandfather Cottman is a hob."

Cottman.

Pip said, "Aha! So your mum is Linda, whose half-brother is Robin Cottman."

"Yes. Have we finished talking about pedigrees?"

"Have you got a pisky kilt?"

"*No.* Neither do I drape myself in a million tonnes of silver. I get the occasional urge for silver, and for billowing grandpa shirts, but I generally make do with the human side, like Dad. He has a silver earring, though. I might get one too as soon as I can be sure it's not just an affectation." He ducked his head, although he wasn't looking at her. "Of course if a pisky maid chooses me and happens to give me one . . ."

"Is that likely?"

He sighed. "Not very. I'd have to spend more time *over there* for that to happen."

"How are the cats?"

If the change of subjects surprised him, he didn't show it. "They're fine, Miss Pearmain. Kittisack has been sleeping on your bed. He implied that was where he always sleeps. Amberjill has been curling up in my bed. She implied that was because it was warm. They're both eating well."

"How about Lupin's cat?"

"He's fine. I've been wiping him down every morning because the other two *will* whisker-wipe him. And before you ask, my dog hasn't done anything to the camomile."

"Good. I hope the lemon tree didn't savage you?"

Jamie said, cautiously, "It tried."

"Hm." Pip gazed out the window. She didn't recognise the scenery yet, but she was sure she would soon.

Jamie had once said she wasn't the napping kind, but the smooth motion of the car made her drowsy.

Pip woke, still in the car, which was now parked under the familiar oak tree in her garden.

She blinked and rubbed her crumpled cheek, hoping she hadn't drooled.

She forgave herself for nodding off. It had been a busy week.

She located her messenger bag and reached for the door-handle, freezing when she glanced at the windshield and saw four eyes gazing at her.

About time, too, Kittisack grumbled.

We have lacked cheese, Amberjill added.

The dog has harassed us, Kittisack said.

Our water bowl has been empty.

We —

"Enough!" Pip cut their Cat-Morse complaint off at the pass. "I'm sure you've been well cared for. You don't *look* lacking, harassed or dehydrated."

Kittisack flipped his tail and leaped off the V-S vehicle bonnet.

We lacked cheese, Amberjill repeated severely.

"Oh, really? You always say that when I'm with you, too. And are you sure you didn't harass the dog first?"

Would we do that?

"Yes. For exactly how long was the water bowl empty? Two minutes while Jamie cleaned and refilled it?"

Amberjill leaped down in the original cat's wake.

Pip shook her head in bemusement. She didn't think for a second that Jamie had been neglecting her housemates. Ergo, they were winding her up, or practising distraction, or something.

She wondered if the dog's testimony might be useful.

Once she got herself and her messenger bag out of the car, she made a quick tour of her garden. Everything appeared to be in fine spirits. Even the lemon tree seemed to be bursting with bitter vim.

"Watch yourself," Pip told it.

Bill the blue-tongued lizard looked up at her from his favourite sunny spot by the woodpile. A few tomato pips and half the shell of a hardboiled egg suggested he'd been well indulged.

The gooseberry grabbed at her as she passed.

"Nice try," Pip said, sidestepping.

The Clancy wishing well looked charming in its corner.

"I saw your bigger brother on an island," Pip said, caressing it.

Was that just this morning?

"And yes, I shall get you a new bucket. I have plans to do decoupage."

She finished her rounds and went into the cottage. It smelled comfortingly of camomile tea, coconut milk, and ginger. Evidently, Jamie cooked.

"Jamie?"

There was no answer, but she heard a faint thumping sound from the bedroom.

"Jamie?" She stepped in and stopped short at the sight of a wicker basket lined with a blanket. In it reposed a chocolate brown dog with curly hair. As it spotted Pip, its tail thumped briefly against the side of the basket.

So that's what I heard.

Pip cleared her throat. "Jamie's dog, I assume? Are you called Chocolate?"

Probably not.

The dog's ears flattened ingratiatingly.

"I don't for a moment believe you started it, but *have* you been harassing the cats?"

The tail went into overdrive.

"Okay, I absolve you." She bent to offer her hand. "You're a fine fellow."

Behind her she detected a Cat-Morsed snigger.

She doesn't know. It was Kittisack.

"She doesn't know what?" Pip swung round.

The original cat and the back-up sat in identical postures with their forepaws together and their tails wrapped around.

"Have you two started colluding?" she demanded.

Maybe. Amberjill sounded coy.

"Well! This is a nice welcome, I don't think! If you recall, you *encouraged* me to go off on my Experience."

Amberjill got up and stretched, strolled over to Pip and whisker-wiped her ankle. *Welcome home, Pippin Pearmain.*

Welcome home, oh marvellous mistress, Kittisack echoed.

Pip frowned at them. "Don't think I don't know what *you* two are. You're fay cats, right? You came through a gateway, though I doubt it was the one *I* weathered."

They blinked at her.

Whatever can you mean? Amberjill narrowed her beautiful golden eyes.

Pip was reminded, ever so faintly, of Jane, delightful, wholesome, sweet-natured and, according to Jules who loved her dearly, habitually manipulative.

No. That's not what he meant. He meant she knows what she wants, and she goes for it in the nicest possible way. How much better than those wishy-washy people who just tread water through life? Brava Jane!

"I met another one of you," she said to the cats.

Amberjill's whiskers twitched.

"Her name was Patchwork Nora."

No twitch.

"She lives with a woman called Branna Pusheen."

No twitch.

"She knows Cat-Morse."

Amberjill didn't quite polish her claws and admire them, but she might as well have.

"Mm-hm," Pip said. She went out to find Jamie.

He wasn't in the cottage, so she went into the garden again. The car was there — no Jamie.

Maybe he'd walked down to Jelly-and-Juice, to flirt with Wanda. Did boys his age still wander down to cafes to flirt with pretty older girls? Or had the tendency been educated out of them? A pity, she thought. She'd quite enjoyed a little flirtation when she was an *older girl*. She still might enjoy some if she found a suitable candidate. Jillian Jules and the gorgeous curly-haired Oash were in their sixties, though they looked much younger. So was Mama Tam, who actually looked her age. *They* evidently hadn't ruled out a bit of sparky interplay. Neither had Liam Dancey, who had been fairly bursting with pride over his water-loving wife and their children.

She sighed.

Jamie had to be somewhere. He'd finished his job, having returned Pip to her place of origin, but he wouldn't have left the car, or his dog, behind.

Maybe she ought to telephone Trip to report his disappearance.

The memory of her hasty triple zero call on *Tulpenmanie* put her off that idea. She didn't want to cause trouble, and Jamie was probably perfectly all right. He was legally an adult, and he was bound to have survival skills full humans lacked.

"Jamie?"

Still no answer.

"Do *you* know where he is?" she asked the cats, who had followed her outside.

Not really, Kittisack signalled.

Not exactly, Amberjill added.

"Some help you are."

Pip went back into the cottage and consulted Lupin's cat.

"Do *you* know where Jamie is?"

Nominally, he's in the bedroom, Lupin's cat replied. He added, *You look well my lady Pippin.*

"Thank you," Pip said, dropping a *reverence.*

She stepped into her bedroom and collided with Jamie coming out.

Pip suppressed a squeak of shock.

Jamie started apologising.

"For heaven's sake! It's all right!" Pip sidestepped him and glanced at the dog basket.

Empty.

"Where's the dog?"

Jamie said, "I don't know."

Pip reached up and poked him in the chest. "Don't start that again, my boy. Where is the dog?"

"I don't —" Jamie caught her inimical gaze and ran a hand through his already rumpled hair.

Kittisack sniggered.

Pip realised she was being unkind. She said, mildly, "Never mind. It's getting on for six. Are you staying for dinner? Or for the night? You're welcome to stay if you have a long way to drive. Or even if you don't. I won't grill you. Much."

"Thanks, but I think I'll get going." He turned, picked up the dog basket and carried it out to the car. In a minute, he was back, collecting up a few things he'd evidently been using.

"I left some soup in the fridge and got a new pack of cat food out of the freezer," he said.

"Thank you. And thank you sincerely for being my driver, and for looking after the cats and the cottage. You've been wonderful. I'm afraid I gave you a bit of a hard time."

He smiled. "You're welcome, Miss Pearmain. I liked being at the cottage, and I'm glad you enjoyed yourself." He headed outside again.

Pip followed. "I had a magical time. And remember, if Jane asks for my address, you are perfectly at liberty to give it to her. That goes for any of the fossmere folk, although I understand some of them can't come through the gate. Why exactly is that?"

"It varies. Waterfolk and treefolk find the water and air here all wrong. Others, such as the leprechaun gossoons, just look too different. Did you happen to meet Liam Dancey?"

"I did. Liffey and Finn presented me to Team Tam, so I met all Mama Tam's . . . um . . . baby dads."

She reflected on those four handsome men, so different in size, face, and form and yet, so she understood, the men Mama Tam thought superior to their peers. One thing they shared, she thought, was an appetite for life. She knew Merryn was married to Jamie's grandmother, and William had told her about his fine wife, Eleanor, who had brought a grown-up son-by-love to the marriage. Only Moss had said nothing about his personal life, but he had certainly not appeared lonely or withdrawn.

Neither am I, she reflected.

"Then you see what I mean," Jamie said.

She nodded. "Master Pendennis is your grandad."

"He is, and we get along well. I don't look like him, unfortunately."

Pip gave him a quick once over. "No, you look like yourself. It's a very good way to look."

She remembered the way Ardal had reacted to her inept attempt to reassure him.

Jamie seemed equally ill at ease, but surely not about *that*. He ducked his head and stuffed his things into the front seat. He stood there, waiting to leave, not quite meeting her eye.

Pip raised her brows. Something was going on here and she didn't know what. It annoyed her.

"Well . . ." Jamie said.

Usually, that meant a prevarication was in the air, but this time it sounded more like indecision.

"Well?" Up went her brows again. It felt odd, as if her face had taken over on its own while her mind was frantically seeking an explanation.

Jamie walked around to the driver's side and opened the door. He slid in and fiddled with the key.

"Aren't you forgetting something?" Pip asked.

"Um—oh!" Hurriedly, he unclipped the cottage door key and handed it to Pip. "I'm sorry. I—"

"You're absolved," Pip said.

More fiddling. "Goodbye then," he said, and started the car.

Pip watched him glance in the rear-view mirror and back out with mathematical precision.

Well, he *was* a quarter pisky . . . and if the mercurial Merryn Pendennis was a typical example, that was a pretty powerful influence that balanced the calm and kindly, if persistent, hob blood. Jillian had said what piskies didn't know about numbers wasn't worth bothering about. Presumably that knowledge extended to mathematics and precise judgements of distance and time.

It's clear I don't have any of it in my genes. Plain old human.

As far as I know, she amended, remembering the distant ancestor who styled herself *Grandmother Aster.* And what was that odd word Branna Pusheen had used?

She watched with interest as Jamie braked, preparatory to pulling into Ribston Lane.

The car eased forward.

Pip stepped up and rapped smartly on the window.

Jamie stopped again, hesitated, and cracked it open. "Yes?"

"Aren't you forgetting something else?"

He glanced at the key.

Pip sighed. "Jamie Pendennis! For the last time, *where is your dog?*"

Chapter Two. Revelations

"I don't—"

"If you say *I don't know* once more, I'll squeal," Pip threatened.

Jamie bit his lip. "But it's true, Miss Pearmain. I don't know where he is, exactly, or where he goes when he's not here. I don't even know where *I* go when I'm not here."

Pip threw up her hands in the dramatic movement she'd used onstage in a play called *Swan*. It had been about a fan dancer, and she'd had to learn the moves in just a few days. She'd always been a quick study.

The hands-up gesture had made an effective ending to Act Two as she'd held the pose, staring straight out into the audience as the feather fans she'd held dropped to the floor before the curtain swished down and she scampered offstage to plunge into the warm chenille dressing gown Sully held ready.

Jamie could never have seen that play, but although less revealing, the gesture was just as effective on him as it had been on the audience.

He dowsed the engine and got out of the car. "We'd better go back into the garden so I can disclose."

Pip followed his upright young back.

She cornered him near the camomile and gave her most ferocious grin. "Right. Dog. Now." Catching sight of the cats watching with interest, she added, "And you two keep quiet.

You had your chance."

Jamie raised his right hand, elbow out, and touched his forefinger to his brow where a cap-brim would have been if he'd been wearing one.

He snapped his hand down and vanished.

Pip had thought herself inured to shocks, having consorted with Jillian, Jules and Tane, and met Liam Dancey, but she squeaked anyway.

She squeaked again as something damp touched her knee.

She looked down, suspecting the cats, and met the soft, apologetic gaze of the curly-coated dog.

Pip sat down with a bump, right in the camomile.

The dog gave a nervous thump of his tail.

He was a lovely dog, really . . . possibly an unclipped poodle. Or something. He didn't smell like a dog.

Pip cleared her throat. "Jamie?"

The dog uttered a soft *wuff* and put a paw on her knee. Then he flopped down, rolled over and the young V-S driver rematerialized before her, lying on his back.

Pip said, "For heaven's *sake,* why didn't you just say?"

Jamie scrambled to his knees and shrugged sheepishly. "It's not the easiest thing to introduce into the conversation. I'm a mutie."

"Mutation?"

"More like mutable. It's Dad's fault, or Grandad Pendennis'. They have the gene too. Some pisky lines do . . . and it sometimes pops up in leprechaun colleens as well."

"Tane?"

"No. Not my sister Laura, either—or they probably do have the gene, but in them it's recessive. It's a bit more common in pisky men, apparently. My great-great grandad had it. *I* shouldn't be able to manifest fully, being only a quarterling, but it happened when I was messing about learning semaphore. Took ages to work out how to come back at all, let alone in my clothes. Dad couldn't help because he does it another way. And Grandad Pendennis just laughed his head off."

"How does your dad do it?"

"Um . . . he touches his foot to the back of his other calf to dog out, and just wills himself back when he's ready. I have to roll over . . ." He grimaced. "You can imagine how much fun *that* was the first few times, going from submissive dog pose to submissive human . . . *bare* submissive human."

"There's nothing to be ashamed of in a bit of bareness."

"I know *that*. But it's not so acceptable in public *over here*. I used to be scared I'd somehow dog out at school and get impounded or . . ."

"Naked under the monkey bars. I do see. Sort of. What's his name?"

"Kakao."

"That makes sense."

He grinned at her. "Possibly. Dad's mutie dog is called Dog Jory — grumpy little fluffy terrier, and Grandad's goes by Unca. He looks like a whippet. Great-great Grandad Jago Pendennis' was called Master Floppy. I think they all let someone else pick their names. I said, since Kakao was *my* dog, I was going to choose the name. Sort of like — "

"Cocoa. For chocolate."

"Yes." He looked pleased. "It's a proper name, not just a descriptor."

Pip contemplated a world which was a great deal odder and much more entertaining than she'd ever realised. Then she said, "So that's why you brought your own bed."

"It doesn't take much space in the boot of the car. I *do* have a bed at home, but I usually sleep in the basket."

"Why?"

"You'll think it's silly."

"You probably think it's silly for someone my age to talk to cats and do ballet practice at seven in the morning after wrestling with an ill-tempered lemon tree."

"I don't, but anyway, it's because I enjoy the dreams he has. They're always happy ones of running through the chalklands *over there*. I—he—we go running with Dad and Grandad Pendennis sometimes. It's wonderful. Kakao dreams of those times."

"Good reason." They got to their feet together, with Pip assisted by his offered hand. "Thanks for telling me."

"Thanks for not laughing."

They stared at one another for a bit longer, then Pip said, "Goodbye, Jamie, and thanks again."

Jamie saluted her, and Kakao trotted over to the lemon tree, cocked his leg, and streaked off through the gap in the wall.

After a few seconds, Pip heard the engine start.

"Well!" she said.

She turned to face the cats. "You two could have explained about Kakao."

We would have, eventually, Amberjill said.

If you'd asked the right question, Kittisack finished.

"As in, is the V-S driver a part-time dog?"

Yes. Asking where the dog is, is . . .

Not the right question.

Because no one has ever worked that out.

Even the dog doesn't know.

Pip harrumphed and headed into the kitchen to seek the soup Jamie had mentioned.

Is the V-S driver a part-time dog? What kind of a person would ever think to ask that?

The soup tasted as good as it smelled, and she ate contentedly, with the cats purring beside her in the expectation of a little chicken and ginger broth being left for them. Evidently they had got over the scratchy mood they'd been in when she returned. Maybe a peace offering of cheese had something to do with it.

After dinner, Pip showered. She'd already done that on *Tulpenmanie*, but at home she could take her time. She went through her usual evening routine and hung up her divided skirt and blouse, now also clean and dry. Then, clad in a rose-pink dressing gown with green trim that used to belong to Little Mum, she opened her messenger bag and removed her bucket list.

Time to add my new bucket.

She paused to picture it as she'd first seen it at Iris's wishing well on Hob's Island.

She'd drunk from it and splashed her face with the soft and sparkling water of *over there,* but the bucket itself had been the prize.

Remembering her last effort at adding to the list, when she'd been in the V-S car heading for who-knew-where, and when no bucket had come to mind, she turned to the page with the ellipsis . . . *to be continued.*

About to begin her entry, she noted a faint shadow under the page and flipped up the pad.

Green writing in modern cursive, not her own, puzzled her for a split second before she remembered Zach had given her a secret in return for hers.

She adjusted her eyes to the larger-formed letters and read.

One night, I was crewing for a company called PitchParties. I jumped off a party yacht – PitchPerfect. I believed the bride-to-be had gone overboard and I was trying to save her. I was almost run down by the boat, and I thought I was about to drown. Someone saved me, by dragging me through an underwater gateway into over there. *That's how I met Jin and how I first went to Hob's Island. Jin handed me over to a fisher maid named Divka, who put me back through the gate. When I surfaced, we had to figure out a pretend rescue, using* Tulpenmanie. *I lost my memories for a while, and so did Jin. It wasn't good. I think some people still believe it was a failed suicide attempt. Later, I met Jin again and we started sorting ourselves out. We're still doing that, which is why we're not engaged.*

Pip stared at the secret as a memory clicked into place. Back when Zach and Jin had been trying to convince her that Tane had merely gone for a night swim in the ocean, she'd been trying to recall the story of someone disappearing in Bass Strait . . . someone more recent than the classic case of Trudy Riley and Debra Finnigan in 1922 and the mystery of Barnabas Singer in 1999. Now she remembered the incident clearly. No wonder the name had seemed a tad familiar when Zach introduced himself.

Zachary Rowan had gone overboard from *PitchPerfect* and there had been a full-on search and an enquiry. The cruise ship company, *PitchParties*, had been exonerated of negligence, but no one, including the eventually rescued Mister Rowan, had come up with a satisfactory explanation for the sequence of events. *Stranded on a Bass Strait island* was more or less what they'd decided.

So, Jin had rescued him and taken him *over there* through that unnerving gateway. That tied in with Jules' comment that Zach's first sojourn *over there* had been unintentional. She wondered exactly what had happened after that, and why Jin hadn't brought him back immediately. Tane evidently knew, but Jules had ordered him not to tell her.

I can always ask Zach directly.

Pip shook her head at herself. She enjoyed eavesdropping on conversations, but asking people outright for their possibly embarrassing secrets wasn't her style.

Except for Jamie and the dog . . . and that's not embarrassing.

She uncapped the pen and wrote up her new bucket in her minuscule script, humming her high mosquito ditty as she went.

After a while, the hum dropped and modulated into "Silk and Circumstance", and she saw dancers in grey costumes moving sinuously across the stage . . .

Bucket first. Ballet later.

She kept her attention on the pleasure of description.

The bucket at Iris's Wishing Well on Hob's Island is made of wood. It's a marvellous bucket of a kind I've never seen before. Like boats and barrels, wooden buckets are made from planks bent into shape, then fixed with bands or glue, but the wishing well bucket was smooth, like driftwood, and I think it must have been made from a single piece of a washed-up tree and hollowed and carved. It doesn't seem damaged from hanging in water, so maybe the wood is something like Huon pine. It was a perfect bucket . . . even better than the Clancy bucket. I wish I could have taken a photo of it, but phones don't work over there, and they can use only the most basic cameras. I'm going to see if I can find a woodturner and ask him, or her, to make me one similar to hang in my wishing well. I've decided to go that route rather than use the decoupage one because I don't know if decoupage is weatherproof. I'll still do one, though.

While the bucket was fresh in her memory, Pip sketched its image into the bucket list. She wondered why she'd never thought to add illustrations before. Maybe it was time to retire the fifty-plus-year-old feint-ruled pad and buy, or make, a dedicated album for the bucket list. She could glue in the original pages with fair copies and add illustrations or photos, and some added context. Jan might know where she could get the relevant supplies.

She could see it now — a beautiful book to be proud of.

Another new project will keep me from feeling . . .

Ouch.

She'd remembered. Lupin had gone to glory, and her gift to Pip had been used up. Pip was home, and tomorrow morning there would be no dancing with Jane on the chalk before slipping into the fossmere to swim, then going foraging with Sulane or finding young Ardal and asking him to teach her to jump . . . There would be no playing with the opinionated Mirri or hearing tiny Tallien go from howling to contented sucking as soon as Jillian raised him to her breast.

Damn it.

Pip sniffled.

She jumped as something pressed against her knees.

The cats had risen in unison to rub their whiskered cheeks on her legs.

Mama Tam's voice murmured in her mind. *You have plenty of love in your life.*

Chapter Three. Monday Morning

April 2022

At a quarter to seven on Monday morning, Pip ventured into the garden.

Bill was still wherever blue tongues went during the night, and the grass was heavily bedewed.

"No nonsense from you," Pip said to the sentient lemon tree as she stepped up to choose her morning victim.

She noted there were few ripe lemons but a lot of shiny green ones. That was April for you. Fortunately, she'd frozen some lemon juice over the summer.

She nipped off a fat specimen lurking under the leaves.

"I hope you enjoyed your nitrogen," she remarked to the tree.

It did, Kittisack informed her. He added, *I have undertaken to squirt my morning libation rootward hereto forth.*

"Why?" Pip asked curiously, strutting back across the lawn with her prize.

Kittisack trotted behind her, placing his paws in her footprints to avoid the worst of the dew. *It seems the right thing to do. The thing might feel deprived now Jamie and Kakao have left.* He paused and added his favourite mantra. *Tell no one.*

"I won't." It was easy to promise that. Whoever would she tell?

At seven o'clock, Pip was already practising. Her call from Magda Saxer was due at eight, and she was certain Magda would be punctual.

Moving her ballet practice forward a little gave her a window to drink her lemon and water before she answered the phone.

She ran through ten minutes of exercises to limber up, then sketched the first entry of the dolphins for the ballet. In her mind's eye, she saw the grey-clad dancers form a circle and move into a series of *jetes*, not simultaneously, but at choreographed intervals to give the impression of the dolphins playing.

There had to be a story, but she'd keep it simple, with play, perhaps an exploration of a sunken ship and a grand scatter when a shark appeared. Or should that be a giant squid?

Pip saw five dancers in close formation, grasping at the fleeing dolphins. Or maybe one, dressed in a costume with long flowing streamers... Then... *aha!* The scatter could take the dolphins through a portal where they would transform into some other creature and dance before slipping one by one back to the ocean and leaving the stage as they had arrived. Perhaps the soloist could be a human swimming with the dolphins and learning their ways.

She sketched movements and visualised scenes.

When her phone pinged the hour, she was sweating, gasping, and ready for a dip in the fossmere.

She had to make do with her lemon and water, but she smiled. So often conceived plans were unworkable or silly, but this one *would* work.

She'd done choreography before, but apart from a few benefit shows she'd never staged it, for the simple reason she had no troupe to hand and no great desire to spend so much time with others.

She still didn't have a troupe, but she *did* have experience teaching dance to children. The people at Apples and Pears might remember. If not, Allie and Angie Blake would.

If she knew where they were.

When she'd thought of them back at the Delmsford Flower Show in February, she'd given up the idea of attempting to find them, but now she had a purpose. Angie had loved dancing, and she'd been surprisingly good at it. Was it too much to hope she might have gone on to have a career in the arts?

Must do a find-me search for Angela Blake alongside dance. She might be a teacher.

She was about to begin the search when her phone rang in her hand.

Eight o'clock.

Magda Quest Saxer.

She'd been expecting the call, but thoughts of her dolphin ballet had distracted her.

"Pippin Pearmain," she said.

"Magda Quest Saxer," her agent responded. She waited a beat and said, "I take it you have considered the offer and come to a decision?"

"I have. I'm saying yes."

"Excellent. Your flight is booked for Wednesday at six o'clock."

Pip's mind screamed at her to retreat, but she said, "Morning or evening?"

"Evening. I gather you're not very close to an airport."

"A couple of hours' drive from the nearest one. More if the traffic is heavy or if there are roadworks."

"That's what I thought. I'll email you the itinerary. I'm coming from Perth, and I should get in half an hour after you. If you have a drink at a bar or a café, we can meet and share a taxi to the motel then head to the studio the next day. Okay?"

"Yes. How—"

"Itinerary coming through now, Miss Pearmain. I'll see you on Wednesday evening."

Pip heard dead air.

She gritted her teeth.

Her new agent had hung up on her—again.

Come back, Sully . . .

Pip rinsed her lemon juice glass and made a cup of soothing camomile tea. She cut cheese for the cats to have after their breakfast.

She'd been going to ask for details, but did she need them? She knew already the trip might last for ten days or more, so she should pack clothing to match that timeframe. Sydney would be a bit warmer than Jellico Bay, but she'd add a light jacket.

Jeans and tops. A smart dress in case she had to impress someone. Comfortable shoes. Toiletries. Underwear and night things.

She began packing immediately, while the momentum was hot. She decided to travel in her divided skirt. She'd discovered already that it was curiously impervious to stains, spills, tears and salt-water dunking. Her matching boots had also proved their stamina.

What are you doing? Kittisack wound around her ankles.

"Packing. I'm going away to test for a part, remember?"

You'll get it.

"I might not. It's been years since I performed."

So?

"I might not be up to it."

You weren't up to riding and swimming and drinking cider with a leprechaun?

Pip had no immediate answer for that. "How did you — oh, forget it. I need to arrange for someone to look after you cats. Should have grabbed Jamie while I had him." She went to her call log to delete the call from her agent and found two missed calls from Friday.

Jan.

Not more bad news.

Her finger hovered over the *bin it* button, but then she reluctantly hit *recall*.

"Pip?" Jan sounded surprised.

"Hello. I found a couple of missed calls . . ."

"You *said* you'd answer your phone or call me back asap." Jan sounded annoyed.

Pip took a couple of metaphorical steps backwards. She *had* promised that.

"This *is* asap," she said.

"Oh? I called three days ago."

"Yes. You left a voucher for me from Lupin when you took off after Clarkia called. It had a phone number for more information, and I rang it then got cornered into *leave now or never* decisions."

"Leave where?"

"For a V-S Experience."

"What did you —"

"Never mind. It's too much to explain. Anyway, my phone was flat after I went overboard, and I finally put it on the charger at nine last night and only just looked at the call log." She puffed out her cheeks. "So, I'm returning your call, asap. Is anything wrong?"

Jan said, "Overboard?"

"Never mind. Is anything wrong?"

"Not *wrong* exactly."

"You must have called for something. And by the way —" She'd remembered how much Jan didn't know. "I've got a screen test on Thursday, and I was wondering —"

"Oh." Jan sounded deflated. "Really? How? Where?"

"My new agent called after you left last week. It's in Sydney, and I hoped —"

"Oh," Jan said again.

Pip started to hum, then stopped abruptly, as she realised the mobile would pick it up. "Jan, what's wrong? Tell me why you called. I won't interrupt."

Jan had been the one doing the interrupting, but she wanted to be tactful.

Jan said, "I was going to ask you a favour."

"Go on." Pip made her voice as welcoming as she could.

"Clarkia needs a place to stay for a while . . . a few days, or possibly a couple of weeks."

It was Pip's turn to say *oh,* and she turned slowly to look at the cats, who sat in good-cat position behind her.

"She can come here, of course," she said.

"But you'll be away."

"Exactly! I was going to ask if you knew anyone who might want to house-sit for me." It was close enough to the truth. "It will work perfectly — that is, if Jellico Bay isn't too far from anywhere for her to be comfortable."

"That's not a problem. She's been living down south and that's *really* out of the way."

"I hope she likes cats," Pip ventured.

"She does. She's a very capable person."

"Perfect. When can she come?"

"Is tomorrow all right?"

"That'll be wonderful. She can pick up on what's needed, and the cats can get to know her before I leave on Wednesday evening."

"We'll see you sometime tomorrow," Jan said.

"Okay. I'll look forward to it. Bye." Pip hung up before Jan could. Then she stared at her phone before returning her attention to the cats.

"Did you have anything to do with this?" she asked.

Not us. Kittisack flicked his tail.

"You said Clarkia would be coming to look after you."

The original cat said nothing, but his blue eyes swivelled to the mantelpiece where Lupin's cat sat surveying the kitchen and its inhabitants.

"So, *you* had something to do with it," Pip said.

I merely passed on some intelligence, Lupin's cat said in his clear Cat-Morse.

"To Kittisack and Amberjill."

Of course.

Pip, aware of feeling sticky and damp, finished her packing and went to shower.

Chapter Four. Clarkia

April 2022

Waiting for someone to arrive *sometime on Tuesday* is never an ideal situation, Pip decided. She'd done some essential shopping on Monday and added supplies to take to Sydney. Sully would have taken care of that, but she thought Magda was a very different style of agent.

She sought Angela Blake plus dance on *find-me* and got far too many hits for Angie as well as Angela.

Many of these hits had photos, but although Pip looked at as many as she could before her eyes blurred, she failed to identify *her* Angie. She'd last seen her at around five years old. By now she'd be nearing thirty. The wavy light brown hair might have turned dark, and it could be any colour or any style. She might have married and changed her surname, but to what?

She found someone called Angel Petty who was a ballroom dancer, but a close examination of her face and figure pulled a blank. This wasn't the right person. For one thing, she was too old.

A search for Chad and Alison Blake brought up a few hits, most of which were clearly about other people called Blake Alison, Chad Alison or Blake Chad. Just one hit seemed a possibility, because it mentioned Delmsford.

That's got to be them.

Her momentary excitement died when she found out it was a kind of old potted bio listed with several others under an umbrella listing of *Project Twenty-Five.*

The date given was sometime in 1997, which fitted in with the timeline she remembered. She supposed she could contact the *Project Twenty-Five* website, but if that was the last information they had about the family, it was as out of date as hers.

I'll try again when I come back from Sydney, she decided. *Or not. After spending days on a filmset – if I get the part – I might not want to go ahead with my ballet after all.*

On Tuesday she did her practice and ran through the routines she'd blocked out already. She wondered if random children from the school would be able to manage even the basic ballet choreography. It might be better to advertise for dancers who had already had some training.

And you think you'll be able to pick and choose? You'll need a venue.

You'll be lucky to find anyone wanting to put in the time. You haven't even asked the school. Do schools let people come in to work with the children now?

She drank her lemon water, made breakfast, and thought wistfully of the family at the fossmere. She was sure it would be easy to round up dancing children *over there.*

It was after nine, but she didn't want to go out in case Jan and Clarkia arrived while she was away.

She settled down with the notes she'd written for Jamie.

At first she thought they might do for Clarkia too, but she soon realised they wouldn't. What *had* she been thinking? She sounded absolutely nuts.

She wrote a new set of instructions, keeping embellishment of headings and numbers to a minimum.

Clarkia
The Cats.
The cats are Kittisack, the Siamese and Amberjill, the calico. They are pretty self-sufficient, but they like their routine.
There is a pack of chicken-and-rice in the fridge. Feed the cats on

the porch using the bowls by the door. Half a cup of food each, at nine in the morning. Wash bowls after use.

A few small cubes of cheese may be given as treats later in the day. Make sure the water bowl, also on the porch, is kept full. They will solicit for anything you're eating. You don't need to give them some, but if they do happen to appropriate human-style food don't worry. They know what is safe for them to eat.

There are more packs of prepared food in the freezer.

The Cottage.

Help yourself to food in the fridge, freezer or pantry, or from the garden.

Lock the door if you leave the cottage and garden during the day or night and remember to take the key with you.

The Garden.

The tall daisies in the garden are camomile and not weeds. Do not prune, mow or uproot them. In fact, no need to do anything in the garden, unless you feel like a bit of light weeding. I have a book on local weeds in the bookshelf if you're unsure about identification.

This cottage is on tank supply. Water is not unlimited.

The blue-tongue who lives in the woodheap is called Bill. He cares for himself. He is friendly. He enjoys tomatoes.

She considered.

If a girl called Jane Pendennis comes to visit, she's a dancing friend of mine. Her friend Ardal might be with her. Another friend called Jamie will probably bring them. He knows the cottage, because he cat-sat for me recently, so you might all have lunch or tea. If anyone else turns up to see me, write down their details. I'll try to text you or call you from Sydney, but I mightn't be able to. You can always leave a message for me with my agent, Magda Quest Saxer. This is her number and her email address. My email address is Pippin_Pearmain AT Sullivan_Gilbert_Agency DOT com.

That seemed to be enough, and besides, she would be able

to tell her everything face-to-face. The note was just a reminder.

Pip took her laptop out onto the porch swing, but she didn't turn it on.

She sat gazing down the garden and wondering if she was making a huge mistake.

She was still sitting there, idly watching Amberjill playing after-breakfast games with the leaves when she heard an unfamiliar vehicle approaching. Since Lemonwood was the last cottage in Ribston Lane, which was a dead-end street, she looked up.

An anonymous-looking silver hatchback nosed in through the gate in the wall and settled next to Pip's little runabout.

She'd been expecting Jan's station wagon.

The driver's door opened, and, after a few seconds, a woman got out.

Jan.

It wasn't. Jan was sixty-four and she looked it. This woman looked more the way Jan had in her wedding pictures. Pip hadn't gone to the ceremony, because she'd been away working on a film called *Ruby Shoes Emporium*, but Little Mum had made an album of pictures.

The woman looked about thirty-five. She had springy brown hair that just missed being ginger, and a broad face. She ought to have been rushing about with a hockey stick or walking a hearty dog, but she looked drawn and sad, as if she'd lately lost weight, and not by choice.

Clarkia. Lord, I hope she's not ill too.

Pip got off the swing and approached the car. Jan was getting out of the passenger seat, but Pip smiled first at Jan's daughter.

"Clarkia! It's a long time since we last met, but I'm Pip." She added, "Welcome to Lemonwood Cottage. These are your hosts, Kittisack and Amberjill." She indicated the cats, who had accompanied her to the car.

To her relief, Clarkia's face relaxed into a smile.

Pip held out her arms. "Give me a hug if you'd like to. I won't be offended if you're not the hugging type."

"For God's sake," Jan muttered. She came forward and hugged Pip herself. Then she stepped back. "My word, you look well!"

"You look—better," Pip said.

Jan did. She must still be grieving for her sister, but the initial shock had obviously worn off. She'd swapped her pinafore for a wrap skirt and a blouse featuring a sunflower print.

Clarkia said, "Hello . . . Pip. I do remember you."

"I'm sorry I haven't made more of an effort to keep in touch with you," Pip said.

"That's okay. Why should you?"

"Because as far as I know, you and your mum are my only living relatives," Pip said.

Clarkia said quickly, "The fact that you *haven't* kept in touch is the reason I'm here. I needed a place to stay, and Mum suggested you. We didn't suppose *anyone* would think of looking for me here. Probably no one but Dad even knows you and I are related, and he won't talk."

Pip glanced at Jan, who put an arm around her daughter.

"It's okay, Mum. Pip needs to know the facts. I'm *not* going to stay here under false pretences."

"Let's go in and get a cuppa," Pip said. She led the way in, with the cats trotting beside her.

"Tea, camomile tea, or coffee? And the loo's through there." She waved her hand.

Jan ducked off immediately, leaving Clarkia to perch on a chair and reach out a hand to Amberjill. "Mum told me about these two."

"You're happy to look after them?"

"Yes. I'll get your vet's number and so on . . . what?"

Pip said, surprising herself, "They don't have a vet. Never

needed one."

Never will, Kittisack said in grumpy Cat-Morse.

"Oh-kay . . ."

Pip said, hurriedly, "They lead a healthy life, and they don't collude with other cats . . ."

As far as I know . . .

"But they've had their shots?"

"I don't know. I didn't have them when they were kittens."

The idea of anyone sticking a syringe in either of the cats was so untenable Pip almost laughed. Instead, she fell to humming.

She was glad when Jan came out. "Tea?"

"Yes please. Clarkia—"

"I'll get my stuff from the car."

Clarkia went out.

Pip made the tea.

Jan glanced up at the mantelpiece and indicated Lupin's cat. "You've still got it."

"Oh—yes." Pip handed over a cup and dug a patisserie box out of the fridge.

"So, you have a part?" Jan asked.

"Maybe. My agent, Sully, went to glory a few days after Little Mum, and the agency never contacted me again. Magda Saxer bought up the contracts and she rang me out of the blue. It's an arty film being shot in New South Wales."

"Do I know anyone else in it?"

"*I* don't know anyone else in it. I mean, I don't have a clue who else might be in it. I'm just going for a screen test."

Clarkia came back in, carrying a laptop bag and a small case. "I brought some work with me," she said.

"What kind of work?"

"Actually—I'm doing some beta reading for Hot Unicorn. That's a publisher." She glanced at Jan.

"I know all about Juniper Gin and her books," Pip said.

"Oh, good."

"I'm waiting on her next manuscript to read myself."

Clarkia put down the case and moved over to the counter. "Do you have herbal tea?"

"Camomile," Pip said. Hadn't she said that already?

"Great." Clarkia seemed to be looking for teabags, but Pip indicated the pot.

"I grow my own and brew it."

They sat around the table, sipping tea.

Clarkia ate half a tart, then put it down and looked levelly at Pip. "As I said, I won't stay here under false pretences. I don't know what Mum told you when she rang."

"Nothing, really," Pip said.

"Okay. I've been living with my partner down south for four years. It's fairly isolated. I was working from home and pulling a few shifts at the Environmental Hiking Centre . . . really just a place where hikers sign in and get maps and information. My partner is an online trader, and he travelled a fair bit. I thought we were on track for the whole thing, not necessarily marriage, but commitment. I suggested we might try for a baby. I didn't want to wait until I was forty then discover the family curse had hit me too."

Pip felt her eyes widen, recalling how she and Jan had speculated about babies.

"Family curse?"

"Low fertility," Clarkia said.

"What — really?"

Jan said, "Probably. Mark and I only ever managed the one, and so did Aunt Rosie. Mum had Lupin and me, but six years apart. Mum and Aunt Rosie were the only children Little Nanna and Little Pop Laurel had, and that was the time of big families of seven or so. They were twins, so it amounted to one pregnancy."

Pip nodded. Maybe there was a practical reason their family had shrunk almost to nothing.

"And of course Lupin and I never put it to the test. At least, I never did . . ."

Clarkia went on, "My partner kept saying, later, and eventually he admitted he already had kids. I assumed it was just one of those things, an early relationship that didn't work out. I even pressed him to get in touch, and to spend time with them. He said they wouldn't know him if they saw him, and their mother had cut ties with him when they were little.

"Then . . . well, the oldest story in the book. Last week, his girlfriend . . . his *other* girlfriend . . . paid me a visit while he was away. She'd found out about me from a *friend* of his. We had a rather tense discussion and a session of show-and-tell. Then she left. So did I." She grimaced. "I was out of there in under an hour. I drove up to meet Mum. He tried to ring me, and I turned my phone off. I finally turned it on again and there were fifty messages to *call me.* And I won't. Nothing he can possibly say will make any difference.

"I brought everything that matters to me along in the car. And before you ask, the girlfriend was not just some random hook-up making trouble. She had photos of them together dating back in their school days, and regular photos covering the years since. She has a matching tatt, and it's not a new one. She—she threw a shirt at me. It was one I got embroidered for him, a joke, with a clarkia flower on the pocket. She has a honeycomb ring that matches one he wears, again not new. I saw the ridge in her finger. He told me his was a ring he got when he was a member of an apiarist club in his teens. Turns out, her name's *Bee.* So—"

"So you want to take some time out at a place he won't look for you," Pip said.

"Right. I got a new phone number. Mum has it, and I'll give it to you and the people I work for, but don't pass it on to *anyone* for *any* reason. Okay? I don't want him, or her, or even their kids calling me, ever. If I ever decide to contact him I'll do it via a solicitor."

"Perfectly okay," Pip said. "Is that your car?" She indicated the door leading out to the garden.

Clarkia said, "No. It's Aunt Lupin's."

"Clarkia thought—we thought—using a different car would cover our tracks," Jan said, smiling faintly. "Very cloak and dagger."

"You'll need it to get home, so Clarkia can use mine while I'm away," Pip said. She glanced at Jan. "Could you give me a lift to the airport tomorrow? It's not far out of your way. And Clarkia, that name of yours is very individual. What's your middle name?"

"Lupin."

"Oh. How about calling yourself Lulu while you're here? You shouldn't need to give your surname to anyone if you pay in cash. If anyone asks, you're my house-sitter, from Purrs and Fur."

"I've never heard of that," Jan said.

That wasn't surprising, Pip thought, since she'd just made it up. "You could order some business cards, or even a tee-shirt. If you enjoy sitting for me, you could *become* Purrs and Fur."

Clarkia and Jan both looked a bit nonplussed.

"Or not," Pip said. She started humming.

Clarkia said, "So *that's* what Aunt Lupin meant."

Pip broke off to say, "Do what you want in the garden, but not to my camomile, and watch out for the lemon tree."

She glanced at Lupin's cat and spoke to it, forming the words in her head.

Will she be all right here with you three cats?

Lupin's cat said, *Clarkia will do splendidly. You have no need to worry about a thing.*

"I'm so glad," Pip said.

"What about?" Jan sounded mildly suspicious.

Pip widened her eyes. "About *everything*."

ABOUT THE AUTHOR

Lark Westerly loves writing series where characters weave in and out of one another's stories.

She also loves playing with ideas and notions and researching odd information.

Lark lives in the island state of Tasmania, where she walks dogs, invents recipes, and rapidly reduces her garments to things that need mending. She rarely wears a matching pair of socks.

Unlike Pippin Pearmain, Lark is not tiny, not an only child, not single and not an on-screen performer. She never learned ballet and she can't speak Cat-Morse. She doesn't even have a bucket list. Nevertheless, Pippin Pearmain and Lark Westerly are sisters under the skin.

Oh . . . you were wondering about that bucket that inspired *Performing Pippin Pearmain*? It happened like this . . .

To find out, visit https://performingpippinpearmain.weebly.com/about-the-bucket.html

www.ingramcontent.com/pod-product-compliance
Lightning Source LLC
Chambersburg PA
CBHW060627130626
46555CB00002B/690